I0670876

HEALING YOU

Hearts of Ridgewood #2

Mia Jade

Mia Jade

Copyright @ 2025 Mia Jade
All rights reserved.
This book is a work of fiction. Names, characters, places, and events are either a product of the author's imagination or used fictitiously. Any resemblance to events, locales, or persons, living or dead, is purely coincidental.
No part of this book may be copied, reproduced, stored in a retrieval system, or transmitted in any form or by any means—electronic, mechanical, photocopying, recording, or otherwise – without prior written permission from the author.

AUTHOR'S NOTE

Healing You is the second and final book for Savannah & Archie, and the second book overall. Some scenes may be disturbing or upsetting, and I strongly advise you to put your mental health first.

Writing Healing You has brought me even further in my writing journey, and taught me things I never thought I needed to know.

Thank you all for staying.

Mia Jade

For the ones who survived.

Disclaimer:

This work contains references to songs, music, lyrics, movies, and other copyrighted material. All such material is the property of its respective owners, and the author acknowledges and respects the copyright of these works.

Trigger warnings: this book contains content that may be disturbing to some readers. It includes themes of abuse, mental health struggles, domestic violence, sexual assault, and descriptions of violence and distressing situations. Reader discretion is strongly advised.

NOTHING IS AN ACCIDENT
JUNE 19TH 2004

SAVANNAH

"There was an accident."

My chest tightened—the kind of aching tension that hits you before your mind even has a chance to process it. Archie's hand faltered on my cheek as I stood up so quickly the world tilted on its axis. His fingers trembled slightly, a crack in his usually steady presence.

I felt nauseous. It wasn't the usual nausea, though. Right now, it felt like my entire body was going up in flames.

I don't remember when I started running.

I heard his voice behind me, calling my name once–sharp, scared. But I was already gone, and he didn't hesitate.

He followed like he always said he would. Not because he understood everything yet, but because he was trying to.

I didn't ask my legs to move. I didn't tell my body to do anything. My body was just a blur of panic and motion, almost as if I was a ghost floating outside my own body.

"Where? Who? Are the boys hurt?" I yelled into the phone, the alcohol ripped from my bloodstream, instantly replaced with adrenaline.

I didn't even register that I was speaking. I just needed answers. Clarity. Something to hold onto before everything slipped.

Archie hovered behind me, and I could feel worry radiating from him. He didn't understand yet, but he could tell that everything was collapsing.

Static cracked on the line. Just for a second. Just long enough for dread to settle like stones in my stomach.

Then his voice returned, shaking.

"They're both dead," he said quietly.

I could hear Aidan's sobs on the other end, and that only split me open further.

Jayden let out a scoff of disbelief before adding, "He fucking finished her off, Savvy."

Archie's hand brushed against my shoulder, then froze. I knew he couldn't hear Jayden. But he could see it in my face. The way my mouth opened. The way the colour drained from my skin.

I blinked. That couldn't be right. My brain scrambled, trying to reshuffle the words into something else. *Anything* else.

My feet faltered.

Mum?

My mum?

"Slow down," I whispered. My voice was paper-thin, almost childlike. My eyes were fixed on the ground, like maybe it would tell me something different. Something kinder. "What happened?"

Jayden echoed, slower this time, like I hadn't heard him the first. Like I hadn't *felt* those words carve themselves into my bones already. "The police said it was a car accident, but we both know nothing is an accident when it comes to him."

Him.

No.

No, no, no.

"Oh my god."

I couldn't breathe. My body was too hot as well as too cold. My ears were ringing. "No, I need- I—" I stammered. All I could do was look up at Archie, wide-eyed and afraid. "I need you."

He couldn't hear Jayden's voice.

But he could hear mine.

And that was enough.

Something flickered in his expression. Shock, maybe. Or something close to reverence.

Because I'd never said those words before. Not like that. Not out loud.

And he didn't say anything, because he knew how much it cost me.

He just nodded. Pulled the keys from his pocket like it was the most obvious thing in the world.

"Let's go."

I don't remember walking to his car or getting into it. I don't remember breathing.

But I remember the way Archie drove.

Like the world was ending.

3

And it sure felt like it was.

My hands were wrung together in my lap, digging into my legs, desperately searching for something real. Something I could *feel.*

But none of it felt real.

Not Jayden's voice still echoing in my ear.

Not the word *dead.*

"Sav." Archie shot me a sidelong glance as he turned onto the freeway, fear written over his face in permanent marker.

I could tell he wanted to ask a thousand things. He was probably thinking about every conversation we'd ever had. Every moment where I deflected. Every obvious sign I'd covered up with a smile.

I knew that face. It wasn't just fear.

It was guilt.

Because now he *knew*—and it was too late to stop it.

"I know you don't want to talk. I know. But I need you to tell me what we're walking into here."

"I don't know," I murmured honestly. My voice sounded like someone else's. My body felt like someone else's. "He killed her," I weakly choked out. "He killed my mum."

Archie didn't flinch, but he didn't look at me again, either. "Maybe not. Maybe it *was* an accident."

I shook my head, tears falling freely now. I hadn't even realised I was crying until I tasted salt on my lips. "Jayden said it wasn't."

"Do you believe him?" Archie's grip tightened on the wheel.

I thought of Aidan's sobs. Of Jayden's voice breaking across the line. Of my mother—

Of my mother.

"I do," I whispered honestly. "But I don't want to."

Saying it only made it real.

I didn't want this to be real.

It couldn't be.

Archie exhaled through his nose, one long breath that sounded like grief or panic or both. His eyes were dark. I could see the weight behind them.

I had finally given him the truth.

After months of pretending. Of silence. Of half-lies and forced smiles.

And now they were just... dead.

They were dead.

No, no, no!

"My mum," I strangled out weakly, my head pressed against the window. "My mum. She's... dead."

Archie made a slight noise from beside me, one that might have been a cry, but I was too broken to lift my head. "Fuck," he muttered beneath his breath, breaking the speed limit beyond comprehension.

It wasn't reckless, just urgent.

We turned onto Chappel Street, my house looking as broken as ever.

But it wasn't.

Because he couldn't break it anymore.

But he broke my mother.

My mother.

Archie didn't waste a moment. The second we were in the driveway, he flung the door open and bolted.

I followed, even though I had no control over my body. I was being dragged forward by some strong, invisible force. Maybe grief. Maybe disbelief.

The next thing I knew, we were both inside.

My house.

My. Hell.

This wasn't happening.

It couldn't be.

Right?

Jayden's red eyes were the first thing I saw when I ran through the front door.

This *was* real.

Jayden didn't cry.

"This can't be right," I gasped, pacing the house, tugging at my hair, trying to wake myself up from this torturous nightmare. "No, Jay. This can't be happening."

"It is." Both of his hands landed on my shoulders, and he tilted my chin, making me look at him. "They are *dead*, Savvy."

The finality in his voice broke something inside of me.

I opened my mouth to speak, but no words came out. Just a sob. And another. And another.

My eyes darted around the room, almost as if I was searching for a sign. A sign that this was all some cruel prank. A sign that I'd been born into a loving family and this was just a long nightmare.

6

I found nothing.

Just three boys on the couch, clinging to each other like a lifeline.

Even Malcolm was holding them tight like he could never dare to let them go again.

I caught a glimpse of something in his brown eyes. Something I hadn't seen in years.

Softness.

That meant this was more than just real.

That meant this was *bad*.

"Do you need anything?" Archie asked the boys, looking more distraught than I'd ever seen him.

As usual, each one of my brothers shook their heads—because that's what we were taught to do.

Don't accept help from anyone.

Archie backed off when he saw the blooming anger in Malcolm's eyes, but in the heaviest of storms, it was nice to see Archie holding it together for us. For me.

"Why is he here?" Jayden asked, voice empty as he vaguely gestured to Archie.

Archie stepped forward, shoulders squared. "I'm not going anywhere. I left her in this bloody house once. That won't happen again."

"You think I'm going to hurt her?" Jayden's head snapped up, anger bubbling to the surface.

"Jay," I whispered, but neither of them heard me.

"I can't trust you," Archie said flatly. "I won't make the mistake of walking away again."

"And you can't swoop in and be the savior," Jayden roared. "It's too fucking late to go back."

I hiccuped a sob, causing both of them to quit arguing and turn their attention to me.

"Savvy," Jayden soothed, pulling me into his warm embrace. "I'm sorry. Fuck."

"How do you know?" I asked, wiping the tears with the sleeve of my hoodie. "How do you know that it wasn't an accident?"

He hesitated before whispering, "She was dead long before the car hit the lake."

Ten words.

That was all it took for my world to shatter before my eyes.

And in that moment, I could barely breathe.

I felt the floor drop out from under me.

My mouth opened. But nothing came. Nothing at all.

"What?" I croaked out, my voice barely audible. "How do you know?"

"There were signs. Defensive wounds. No water in her lungs. She didn't drown, Savvy. He killed her before the crash."

Murdered.

That word was flashing through my mind. It made my skin crawl.

Before the crash?

Oh my God.

She would have spent so long without air in her lungs. So long begging him to spare her life.

It had been a rare occurrence over the course of my life for me to feel more sympathy towards my mother than anger—but tonight was an exception.

Tonight, I knew she was just a child once.

"Don't… say any more," I whispered, my hands turning numb. "Please."

Archie muttered a string of curses under his breath before asking, "Why would he—"

"Why wouldn't he?" Jayden's voice was colder than ice. "It was always gonna be someone."

"Don't say that," Archie said.

"He's right," I muttered, finally letting out a breath. "We were never all going to make it out alive."

Archie went silent, blowing out a shaky breath. "What happens next?"

Jayden looked older than he should have as he said, "We go into foster care. They split us all up and throw us into homes with families who don't give two fucks whether we live or die."

I'd always known that word was lurking in the background. *Foster care.*

But hearing Jayden say it made it solid. Made it final.

We were going to be ripped apart.

Strangers in strange homes.

And I wasn't ready to lose anyone else.

"Jesus," Archie murmured, taking a thoughtful pause. "I can help."

My head snapped up, still sniffling. "What?"

"My mum's a lawyer," he explained carefully, almost as if it was just dawning on him. "She placed Billy into foster care years ago. She can make sure you get a good family."

Jayden's eyes widened slightly, glancing at me before locking eyes with the boy I was admittedly falling in love with. "I can't ask you to do that. I can fix this on my own."

"You can't." I heard myself say. "Let him help. Jayden, just this once, let somebody help."

He sighed, clearly defeated. "I can't pay you back for helping us."

"I know." Archie nodded, grip tightening on my hand. "I didn't go into this blind, and I don't expect anything in return."

I managed a weak smile through the tears. "Thank you."

Malcolm approached then, face utterly blank. "Where are we staying tonight? Aidan needs fucking sleep."

"You can stay with me," Archie insisted, shooting me a glance of concern. "Until we figure out the rest of it. We have spare rooms."

Jayden looked at Archie with a mix of exhaustion and distrust, but his expression visibly softened when he caught a glance of Aidan and Leo curled up on the couch. "We don't have anywhere else to go," he murmured, rubbing his eyes. "Thanks."

I didn't know how to feel about any of this.

It had been so easy earlier tonight. And then everything just... crumbled. So quickly. So *violently*.

I couldn't make sense of it.

My father, my worst enemy, was dead.

My mum was dead.

Foster care.

Strangers.

This was exactly why I'd been so hesitant to let Archie in. I thought he would get caught up in my mess. And he did. He *did*.

I had warned him, hadn't I?

Maybe I'd never said it loud enough, but he knew. He knew I was a storm dressed in human skin.

I didn't want to do this to him. Destroy him. He had a bright future ahead of him, and we both knew it. Me? I could hardly picture tomorrow.

But then he looked at me with a mix of devastation and softness, and I realised I needed to let him in. Maybe that was the only way forward.

"Thanks," I said quietly. Numbly.

I could barely feel anything, but I knew the boy next to me, and I knew he'd changed my life. *Saved* my life.

My phone buzzed then.

Eighteen missed calls.

Four from Liv. Five from Izzie. Two from Josie. Three from Danny. One from Billy. Three from Theo.

Fuck.

I couldn't handle this.

I couldn't explain my sudden disappearance, because that would mean explaining years of secrets.

I could barely take a breath without it hurting.

"We should go." I heard Jayden whisper. "Deal with the rest… tomorrow."

Drawing in a sharp breath, I put my familiar brave face on and pretended my world wasn't falling apart right in front of me.

But even though it was—I had Archie right by my side. Not out of obligation. Out of *choice*.

BROKEN HOMES, BROKEN GIRLS

JUNE 20TH 2004

ARCHIE

She was broken.

She was so fucking destroyed and there was nothing—*nothing*—I could do about it.

I held her for hours. I didn't know how to fix it. I didn't know *if* I could. She was sobbing uncontrollably for hours, and fuck, I'd never seen somebody so devastated. She made silence loud. Every breath of hers was a scream muffled in my chest.

I wished I could carry her pain. Take it all in so she could breathe. But grief isn't a weight you can share. It's a void that swallows you whole.

I watched her unravel, helpless to do anything but hold her through it. I kept thinking back to the support I needed when I lost my dad and Elsie, but nothing helped.

I remembered sitting alone in my room after Dad's funeral, the silence pressing in like a physical thing. Elsie's laugh had stopped, and with it, the light in the house. I had wanted someone to reach in and pull me out of that dark, but no one came.

And I needed to. For her.

Sav had been shaking so hard, almost like her soul wanted to leave her body. I'd never hated the world more.

I couldn't stop picturing her face. Every time I closed my eyes, there it was. The vacant look. The trembling hands. The red eyes that looked like they were no longer seeing the world, but living inside of a memory.

No, not just *a* memory. A nightmare. One she couldn't wake from. One I couldn't pull her out of.

I'd never been so distraught over a sight before.

Honestly, I don't know how I kept my shit together. I was so close to losing it with her.

The smaller boy, Aidan, had attached himself to me. Even now, at three in the morning, he was clinging to my leg like I was the only thing keeping him tethered to the earth.

Damn it. One day.

That was all it took.

I clenched my fists, remembering the last time I felt this helpless. The way Dad's smile had faded, the way Elsie's laugh had gone quiet. Back then, I thought I had time to fix things. But grief doesn't wait. It just arrives and takes hold.

How many times had I promised to be stronger? To not let the people I cared about fall apart? And yet here I was, failing all over again.

One glance at the Greys, and I could see it clear as day.

And all I could think was: *How the fuck did I miss this?*

Her mum's reaction when I was in their house. The bruises I saw before Marlee's memorial. The way Sav always kept a part of herself locked away.

I *should* have seen it.

I should've been better.

God, she trusted me. Against all odds, she put her trust in *my* hands. And I didn't see what was happening right in front of my face.

She'd been hiding in plain sight, and I hadn't looked hard enough.

I wanted to scream. Throw something. Tear this entire broken system apart with my bare hands.

But I couldn't.

Because there were six kids in my house right now, and not one of them had anybody but each other.

And me, apparently.

Whether I was ready or not.

I looked around my bedroom, dark and quiet and fucking lonely. Leo had fallen asleep on the pull-out couch. Jayden was sitting on the floor, head tipped back against the wall, eyes open but distant. Malcolm was still awake, too. He'd been pacing in the next room like a lost animal for the past hour.

We had plenty of spare rooms, but nobody wanted to be separated tonight. I didn't blame them.

I lived in a big house. I knew that. But the amount of bodies in one home—each of them haunted and afraid—made it feel like a small cottage.

When Billy was getting tossed from one shitty home to the next, Mum fought for him until he had a place that actually stuck.

She could do that again.

I was certain of it.

But even knowing that, I still didn't want to let Sav out of my sight.

Not today. Not tomorrow. Never again.

I reached for her hand, fingers trembling, afraid that if I let go, she'd vanish into the dark forever. Her fragile breathing was the only anchor I had left.

"Archer?" That was Mum. "Will you join me downstairs?"

I glanced over at Sav, curled up beside me on the bed, her breathing finally even, but a frown etched on her face like she was fighting off the nightmare.

I gently peeled Aidan from my leg, tucking him in next to his big sister. I pulled the blanket over them both, Aidan's fingers staying curled around my hoodie until the last minute.

I knelt down beside Aidan, the little guy's eyes barely open.

"You okay, mate?" I whispered.

Aidan nodded slowly, clutching my hoodie tighter.

"I know it's scary. I feel it too. But you're safe now."

He yawned, the tension in his small frame easing just a bit.

For the first time tonight, I let myself hope maybe we could all be safe. Together.

Once I was sure he'd fallen back to sleep, I stepped into the hallway, closing the door behind me as quietly as possible.

Mum was by the stairs, looking more exhausted than ever.

"What is it?" I asked quietly. "Did you hear something?"

Her expression softened. "You need to let me deal with that side of things."

"That side of things?" I echoed, brows drawing together. "Christ. The girl was being abused the entire fucking time I knew her and I didn't even see it!"

Mum didn't flinch. She didn't correct my language. Just nodded, her eyes full of that quiet, knowing grief.

"I know," she said quietly. "It's devastating."

"It's more than devastating." I shook my head, the words tumbling out. "These kids have *no one.* They only have each other. You have to find them someone good. Really good."

"That's always the goal, Archer."

"No," I snapped. "This is *Sav.*"

She paused, watching me carefully. Then, almost like she couldn't stop herself, she smiled. "I'm beginning to think she means more to you than you let on."

I didn't even try to deny it.

17

"She does," I said quietly, running a frustrated hand down my face. "She really fucking does."

Mum sighed, crossing her arms, her tone a little more business-like. "Then you'll be glad to hear I've found a potential family. Nothing's locked in yet, but I've started the process."

My chest tightened. "Already? Who?"

"Adele and Jason Wynter," she said. "You can't say anything to the kids yet. It's early. But they're interested."

"Wynter," I repeated, the name tugging something at the back of my brain. "Do we know them?"

"I do. Lovely couple. They've got a daughter Savannah's age, Brooke Wynter." She frowned, deep in thought. "Riley's girlfriend."

"Riley's girlfriend?" I repeated, clicking instantly. "Wait, *they* want the kids?"

She nodded. "Yes. All of them. Siblings together, which is rare. I know you aren't always fond of the guys on your team, but—"

"Do you think that matters at all right now?" I stared at her, voice hollow. "If you didn't notice, this is all royally fucked up."

"Archer," Mum warned, sighing. "Of course I have noticed. I currently have six extra children in my house, all of which are battered and bruised."

"Sorry," I muttered. "I just-"

"I know."

There was a moment of silence before Mum headed to the kitchen, pouring herself a glass of water. "The funeral is on Tuesday," she whispered. "Their grandmother called me."

I nodded slowly, processing her words. Funeral. *That word always hits different.*

"What do I do?"

"You *stay*," she said gently, rubbing a soothing hand down my back. "You be who you needed."

My head snapped up. "What?"

"When you lost your father. And Elsie," she said slowly, visibly wincing at the memory. "I wasn't there for you the way I should've been, and I apologise for that. But you... you know what grief feels like. What it looks like in a young person's body. Use that."

"So... I go to the funeral?"

"You ask Savannah if she wants you to go to the funeral." Mum offered me an encouraging smile. "Whether she does or doesn't, you offer the support you could have used."

My throat tightened. I remembered standing in that church in year seven, dressed in black, everyone too afraid to speak. I remembered the flowers wilting on her coffin and the way the world didn't feel real for months – or years – afterward.

Grief makes you grow up, but not in a way people can see.

It's not like getting taller. It's like getting heavier.

Like you're dragging a version of yourself behind you that no one else can see.

That boy I was at Elsie's funeral? He still lives in me. Every time someone else breaks, he wakes up again.

I blew out a shaky breath, resting both elbows on the bench. "I can do that."

Because I also needed that person. I still did. Grief doesn't leave – it just settles into your bones. Whether you like it or not, grief always has a way of making itself at home. Haunting you forever.

I looked back up the stairs, heart in my throat. She was up there, barely holding on.

And maybe I couldn't save her.

But I could try.

So, now more than ever, I needed to place all my cards down with this girl.

And if she let me stay, I would.

Now and forever.

No half-in. No second thoughts. Just everything I had left.

Being around this girl was by far the hardest—and the best—thing I'd ever done.

"When Elsie died," Mum began, her voice barely above a whisper, "I didn't know how to be there for you. I thought... if I pretended to be strong, maybe you wouldn't see how broken I was. But that was wrong, wasn't it?"

I swallowed hard. I wasn't used to her saying Elsie's name out loud. It felt like dust on a shelf – something once precious, now untouched.

"Yeah," I choked out. "That was wrong."

"I'm endlessly sorry, Archer." Mum smiled weakly down at me. "I never meant to make it worse for you, and I am sorry that's how it went down."

"All good, Mum," I said back, and I meant it.

Because, really, I could never blame her for the events of that year. We were both grieving.

Mum gave me a soft squeeze on the shoulder before climbing back up the stairs, leaving me alone in the silence.

But now? The silence didn't bring me back to that night.

The silence just made me think deeper about the way one girl had managed to fucking rewire my brain chemistry in the matter of months.

I stayed where I was, elbows pressed to the counter, hands still trembling.

It was nearly pitch black downstairs, the only light from the fridge reflecting onto the floor.

I was about to head upstairs when I saw him. Jayden.

He stood in the doorway, arms crossed, eyes rimmed red but still sharp. "Didn't think you'd be the type to mope in the dark," he said dryly, pouring himself a glass of Coke.

I glanced up. "Didn't think you'd be the one to come down for a chat."

He shrugged, slowly sipping his drink. "I didn't come down for you."

"Right," I murmured.

Still, he didn't leave.

Instead, he circled around the bench and sat in the chair beside me, body limp like the weight was too much to hold up. His eyes flickered to the roof, gaze fixed like he could see right through.

"She's sleeping," I said.

"I know." His voice was low. Exhausted. "She hasn't slept well in a long time. Not unless she's…" He vaguely gestured to me, looking a bit disturbed. "Not unless she's with you, I guess."

I didn't say anything.

Jayden let out a sharp breath. "I used to think you were just some rich kid playing white knight. You always were known as Ridgewood's man-whore."

I didn't argue. Couldn't. "Maybe I was."

He leaned back in the chair, watching me with newfound curiosity. "You still in it? Or is this where you bail?"

I met his eyes. "She's not just some girl to me. I'm not going anywhere."

His eyes narrowed slightly, like he was checking for cracks in my armour. "Good," he whispered. "I can't always be there to protect her. Not when I have the boys to worry about, as well."

"You don't have to protect everybody," I told him, and it was the most honest thing I'd said all night.

He went quiet, then scrubbed a hand down his face and muttered, "I don't trust easily. You probably figured that out."

"Yeah, I did."

Another pause. Then: "But I don't think you're full of shit anymore."

I huffed a laugh. "High praise," I replied. Then, quieter, "I don't *not* trust you with her."

He nodded. "I know."

He smirked. I smirked back. *Look at us. Bonding.*

Don't get me wrong, it was painful and awkward. But still bonding.

"She's had it proven time and time again that good things don't always last," he admitted. "I need her to know that it's not *always* temporary."

"She's a strong girl," I replied with a half-smile. "She'll figure it out," I promised. "Maybe if we stop being dicks to each other long enough to show her we've got her back."

His head snapped up. "Don't say we."

I chuckled, scratching my jaw. "I know you're always gonna be there for her. But I've just joined the team."

He snorted. "Not sure I like that metaphor."

"Too bad," I shot back. "We're teammates now."

He chuckled – actually chuckled.

He didn't run off, didn't shoot it down. He didn't threaten to punch me, which felt like *major* progress.

"You should get some sleep," I told him. "Especially if you're gonna survive Tuesday."

"Right." His smirk faded a little as he stood up. "The funeral."

He nodded and stood up, heading for the stairs. As he reached the bottom step, he glanced at me over his shoulder. "She likes you, you know."

I raised an eyebrow. "What?"

Jayden shrugged like there was no need for words. Maybe there wasn't. "Don't fuck it up."

I didn't say anything. Just nodded. It was the closest thing to a blessing I'd get from him.

And then he was gone.

Jayden's words echoed in my head, but beneath the tiredness was something fierce. I wasn't just some rich kid anymore. I was part of this broken, messy family now. And that meant fighting. For Sav. For the kids. For the scraps of hope left in the darkness.

FLOWERS ON FLOWERS

JUNE 22ND 2004

SAVANNAH

My mother never liked flowers. She always said they died too quickly.

But today, the church was full of them.

Lilies. White roses. Sunflowers. All of them were soft, delicate, *wrong*.

It was ridiculous, really.

Gentleness couldn't erase what had happened.

Having a joint funeral for the two of them felt wrong on many different levels. The man who made her life hell, who hurt her, who *murdered* her, had no right to be missed.

It felt like somebody was trying and failing to cover up a wound with lace.

I slid into the last empty seat in the front row, directly between Jayden and Malcolm.

Leo was further back with our grandmother, a woman we hadn't seen in years. She had a thick grey braid down her back and tired eyes that didn't quite meet ours.

I hadn't even known she was alive.

She was our father's mother, which explained everything. I assumed he did something cruel, something final that led her to shut him out forever. I understood – I really did – but knowing that she never came once for us, never knocked on the door or sent a letter even though she knew the house we lived in… it still stung.

Aidan wasn't here at all.

He was considered 'too young' to attend a funeral—as if grief had an age range.

Aidan's birthday was yesterday. He turned three. He spent the day waiting by the front door, holding the little blue truck neither of them ever noticed he loved.

And while our parents had never made his birthdays one to remember, it was devastating to see his little face waiting for people who'd never come.

There are some wounds you're not supposed to have at three.

Archie's mum had agreed to watch him until the service was over. Until I was thrown into some stranger's home and told to settle in.

But at least I wasn't being separated from my brothers.

That was all I ever wanted.

To keep them safe.

Archie came with me today.

Of course he did.

He was in the back row with the rest of our friends, but I could feel his presence from here, impossible to ignore. Just like gravity.

Apparently, his mother found me a lovely family. I didn't know what that meant, or how lovely you had to be to take in kids this broken. But Archie looked right into my eyes when he said it.

I knew he would never lie to me.

Especially about this.

He knew what was at stake.

Me.

My brothers needed and deserved stability.

Then again, so did I.

Still, I had to survive this part first.

And god, I hated this part.

This hour. This church. This moment.

The pastor's voice was steady but distant, like it was underwater. I caught maybe every third word. Something about grief, then healing, then leaving behind pain and stepping into the light.

Fuck the light.

I didn't want light. I wanted the truth.

I couldn't stand sitting here and listening to this stranger pretend my father was a good man. Couldn't look up and ignore the photo of my mother by the front. She was only a baby in it, roughly thirteen. Before *he* got to her. Before everything went black.

How dare they gloss over that?

My fists clenched in my lap, nails biting into my palms.

I heard Malcolm's breath hitch beside me. He wasn't crying, just... hardly breathing. He was holding it all in, and I didn't know whether to envy him or be scared for when it all came spilling out.

When it was time to carry Mum's coffin, there was an awkward shuffle. No one moved at first.

There were no family friends.

No neighbors who'd come with cakes.

No friends offering support.

She'd been alone long before her death.

Our father?

He'd had plenty of people willing to carry his.

Some of them even laughed while talking about him.

I nearly vomited in my mouth at the memory.

After the priest stood by the coffin, Jayden rose slowly, face pale, jaw clenched.

I thought he might pick one of the funeral staff, or distant friends we couldn't recognise.

But his gaze drifted past them, and landed on Archie.

Jayden wanted Archie to help?

Archie stood up immediately, nodding without needing an explanation. He moved toward the aisle, and Jayden gave a small, grateful exhale before looking at Theo.

Theo, he always found somewhat interesting. Well, he found him weird, but Jayden knew he would show up when it counted. I wasn't sure when their unlikely bond had formed, but it happened.

"Theo?" Jayden whispered, voice almost breaking at the end.

"Say no more." Theo offered him a tiny smile of support. "I'm here, bud."

Jayden gave him a nod, relief flicking in his eyes for a split second.

Danny came forward next. He didn't wait for an invitation. He simply stood, clapping a hand on my brother's shoulder. "I'll help," he told Jayden, in that low, calm tone that always came out when he cared.

With the priest, that left one spot.

Jayden glanced at the back row again. His brown eyes darted around for a moment before landing on Billy.

Billy looked at me first.

Always asking permission. Even now.

I gave him the tiniest nod. It was all I could manage.

He let out a slow breath, stood up, and walked forward to join the others.

Together, the six of them lifted my mother's coffin.

The silence as they moved was almost unbearable.

I couldn't cry.

Not because I didn't want to.

Because if I started, I wouldn't stop.

I felt somebody land in the chair beside me once it was empty, just before I felt a familiar pair of arms wrap around me.

"You're not alone." That was Liv. "I've got you."

Josie slid in on my other side a moment later. Her hug was tighter. Josie and I weren't quite as close as Liv and I, but that never mattered.

She was always there.

"I never noticed," Josie whispered into my hair, voice shaking slightly. "I'm so sorry I never noticed."

She knew?

Did they all know?

For a second, the shame curled in my gut. Then it passed.

The man who would punish me for speaking the truth was dead.

And I felt nothing but relief.

Horrible, aching, *liberating* relief.

Izzie didn't hug me, just hovered over us. That was enough. I knew she loved me, she just wasn't sure how to show it.

Plus, she was here – in a church, of all places – even with every bit of her childhood trauma screaming at her not to.

I hadn't expected her to come, but I appreciated it more than I knew how to tell her.

I'd thank her for it someday.

The coffin passed by us slowly, carried by boys who'd all grown up too fast. Jayden's face was like stone – but I knew what was behind it. The hope he never let die, the way he always tried for Mum.

Now she was gone.

Archie's eyes locked on mine for a split-second as he passed by, and I could see the way this gutted him too.

Not for her.

Certainly not for dad.

But for *me*.

Because he knew all too well how haunting parental death could be.

The doors opened. It was grey and drizzly outside as they carried her coffin.

And just like that, she was gone.

My mother.

Forever.

I stayed sitting after the doors closed, even as everyone began to move.

Somewhere in the distance, the pastor thanked everyone for coming, like this was a school play or a piano recital.

We had two hours.

Two hours until we were thrown into a foster home with parents who, most likely, just felt sorry for us.

Apparently, they found our story upsetting.

Our story. I almost laughed at that.

It wasn't a story – it was our lives.

Malcolm stood next to me, one hand tugging at the sleeves of his suit like he wasn't quite sure what to do with his body now that it was over.

"Are we supposed to do anything?" he asked in a murmur. "Like, say something, or…"

I shook my head. "There's nobody waiting to hear from us."

Harsh? Sure.

But it was the truth.

And Malcolm had been around long enough for me not to sugarcoat these things.

He nodded slowly, like that made sense. Like it always had.

In a way, it had.

Nobody had ever been waiting to hear from us.

Jayden stepped back into the row, squeezing my hand once before clearing his throat. "You alright?" he asked.

I hated that question.

What answer could I possibly give that wouldn't break us both?

"I don't know," I whispered. "Still here."

His jaw clenched right as he let out a bitter laugh. "That's something."

Josie gave me another quick hug. "You want me to come with you?" she asked. "In case the new family is like... full of serial killers? Or just for moral support."

I blinked. "You'd actually do that?"

"I've got my bag in the car," she said. "Just say the word."

I couldn't tell if she was joking, but I wanted to say yes so badly it physically hurt.

Instead, I just smiled. "Thanks, but I should do this one on my own," I replied. "Lovely family might not want a plus-one."

"I'm proud of you," she said.

I didn't know what to do with that.

What was there to be proud of? I hadn't done anything. Hadn't saved my mother. Hadn't saved Marlee.

I was just left to pick up the pieces.

Again.

I offered her another hug before following my brothers outside.

Archie was already waiting by the railing, his jacket soaked but his hands jammed into his pockets like he couldn't feel it.

"You didn't have to help," I told him once I reached the gate.

His eyes cut toward me. "Yes, I did."

Silence.

Just for a moment.

"You helped," I whispered, feeling grateful. "I mean... obviously, you helped. But just... thanks."

He looked away. "Still feels like I dropped something."

Me. He meant *me*.

"You didn't," I said, voice sharper than I meant.

He turned back to me, green eyes scanning mine. "I know I didn't. But I also know you're not okay. You're standing here like you've got a plan, but you do not have a plan."

"A plan for what?"

"For anything," he replied, voice softening slightly. "You don't have a plan. You think you do, but you don't..." He trailed off, jaw clenching. "You don't know how hard this will be."

"Grief?" I raised an eyebrow. "I know very well how hard grief is."

"I know." He nodded in understanding. "But this isn't the same. They're your parents. Now you're going into foster care."

"I know," I muttered, realisation dawning on me.

I knew all of these things.

But, God.

They were scary.

He sighed, reaching out to hold my hand. "I'm just saying you don't need to be strong all the time," he explained. "You're allowed to fall apart every now and then. Nobody deserves that right more than you."

AT LEAST I'M TRYING

JUNE 22ND 2004

SAVANNAH

"Can you knock?" I asked Jayden, tightening my grip on Leo's little hand. "Please?"

Jayden nodded stiffly, his movements cautious as he stepped toward the front door of our new house.

It was a towering, almost intimidating thing with large windows and the kind of polished beauty that you saw in movies. It was almost too massive, too perfect for people like us.

But this was our life now. Supposedly.

So, he knocked.

I adjusted Aidan on my hip as Leo's grip tightened on my hand. Jayden and Malcolm each took a step back, jaws clenched like they were waiting for a punch. Maybe we all were. We didn't know what we were walking into here. Another toxic environment, a temporary stay.

I wanted to believe this was different. That this wasn't just another house with a timer ticking down above the door, waiting to eject us the second we misstepped or said the wrong thing.

But I'd thought that before.

I didn't remember it until we found out we were going back into foster care—but we'd done this before.

It was a short stay, back when I was nine. A month in, they gave up on us. That Aidan cried too loudly, that Leo didn't speak enough, that Malcolm was "withdrawn," that Jayden "had anger issues."

They never said what *I* was. Just left a post-it note with "sorry" stuck to my duffel bag.

So yeah. Hope?

Hope was dangerous.

Still, I clung to the last piece of it, praying it wouldn't die again.

The knock echoed for a second, like the house itself wasn't used to being disturbed.

We waited. I thought maybe no one would come. Maybe they saw us through the window and decided we weren't worth the trouble.

Then, it opened.

A woman stood in the doorway, maybe mid-thirties, with long brown waves and soft blue eyes that somehow managed to be both piercing and warm. She gave us a smile then, not the same smile most people offered, the one that made us feel like skittish animals, but a real one.

"You must be the Greys." Her eyes landed on me. "Savannah."

I cleared my throat, eyes widening slightly. "Um, yeah. Hi."

"Hello," she replied softly, eyes flickering back up. "I'm Adele."

Her voice was gentle, warm, like maybe if she spoke in any other way, we would bolt. Maybe we would've.

Behind her, a man appeared. Slightly taller than her, broad shoulders and a kind face that looked like it knew both heartbreak and how to fix a broken fence. His hair was a similar shade to his wife's, but his eyes matched mine almost perfectly.

"I'm Jason," the man explained, offering us all a smile, less bright than Adele's, but still genuine. "Why don't you guys come in? You're safe here."

That word was a weapon when misused.

Safe didn't just mean locks on doors and warm dinners.

It meant knowing no one would yell when you spilled juice.

It meant being able to sleep without one foot on the ground, ready to run.

I wanted to believe Jason. His eyes looked kind. But I'd learned kindness could wear masks too.

I glanced at Jayden, and he gave me a small nod. He entered first, steps slow and deliberate, before I followed with the boys.

The house was seriously beautiful. There were bookshelves covering the majority of the walls, and that brought me comfort in a way I never expected. It smelt a mix of lavender and cinnamon, which was better than whiskey and drugs. So, so much better.

There were pictures on the wall, but not fake ones. Back home, our photos were either the ones that come in the frame, or they were smashed. But these ones? They were real. Raw. Adele with a messy bun, maybe a few years ago, pushing a child on the swing. Their engagement. Their wedding day.

It was comforting.

"Wow," Malcolm muttered, just behind me. His voice was low but filled with something like disbelief. "They're real people."

That made my heart crack a little.

A girl appeared at the top of the stairs then. She froze when she saw us.

Her brown hair was tied into a braid, grey eyes staring back at me like a mirror. Yeah, something weird was happening.

"Hi," she whispered, raising an eyebrow slightly. "I'm Brooke."

I offered her a polite smile. "I'm Savannah. This is Jayden, Malcolm, Leo, and Aidan," I explained, gesturing to each of the boys as I did.

"Do you go to Ridgewood?" I asked. I'd definitely seen her somewhere.

"Yeah." Her smile stretched wider as she finally made her way down the stairs, eyes softening when she saw Aidan in my arms. "You do too? I think I've seen you."

I nodded. "Yeah."

After a few moments of silence from all of us, Jason cleared his throat. "Brookie, why don't you show them to their rooms?"

"Oh, yeah," Brooke said, gesturing for us to follow her. "Come with me."

I exchanged a glance with Jayden, and he shrugged like, *Might as well.* We followed her up the staircase, the boys trailing behind like ducklings.

The banister was smooth, not at all worn or covered in marks. A sign that maybe, just maybe, this family could give us stability.

Once we reached the top, the hallway was bright and open. Brooke walked ahead of us, pausing at the first bedroom in sight. "This one's for Aidan and Leo. We put the beds next to each other. I thought they might sleep better that way?" Brooke explained, but it sounded like more of a question.

Jayden nodded stiffly, clearing his throat. "They will."

Brooke exhaled a sigh of relief as we followed her into the room.

The room was painted a soft blue colour, with little blue stars stuck on the ceiling. Two matching beds with navy covers sat side by side, and in the corner, there was a tiny shelf already perched by the window, filled with toys and books.

I hadn't realised I was holding my breath until then.

Maybe it would seem small to other people, but not to me. Every colour-coded bookshelf, every poster on the wall, every stroke of paint – I felt it so deeply.

Because someone had looked at this room and thought of my brothers. Thought about what might help them sleep.

No one had ever done that before.

Leo reached up and grabbed my hand, brown eyes wide. "This is ours?"

"Yeah, baby," I said softly, feeling a deep surge of happiness for him. "It's yours."

"Huh." Malcolm grinned, still in the hall. "This is actually nice."

Brooke smiled like that was the nicest compliment she received all week. To be fair, Malcolm wasn't exactly known for his heartfelt words.

Leo took Aidan into the room, instantly digging through the multiple toy boxes.

The rest of us followed Brooke to the second bedroom, stopping just in front of the door. "This one's Jayden's," she told us before gesturing to the one next door. "And that's Malcolm's."

Malcolm nodded once, stepped inside, and closed the door without a word.

Jayden gave me a look. "He'll warm up," he said, disappearing into his own room.

Brooke laughed quietly. "Do you mind sharing a room with me?" she asked then, nervously fiddling with her fingers. "I would have given you your own, but I figured Jayden and Malcolm wouldn't want to share, so…"

"That's all good." I smiled despite myself. "I'm happy to share a room."

Relief washed over her face. "Amazing."

I followed her to the end of the hall, and we entered the biggest bedroom besides the master. It was... flawless, to say the least.

Again, there were a few bookshelves against the walls, a wide window with a view of a park, and two queen beds perched in the middle.

Jesus.

I'd never seen anything like this, let alone been allowed to stay.

"Your house is really pretty," I told her with a smile.

"*Our* house," she corrected, opening her wardrobe to reveal an empty half. "I cleared out some of my stuff so you'd have room for clothes."

Before I could say anything, I saw a boy around our age watching us through the window. "Do you know him?" I heard myself ask.

Brooke's whole face changed. She yanked the blinds shut. "*That* is my sometimes boyfriend."

"*Sometimes* boyfriend?" I tilted my head to the side.

She sighed, flopping on the bed closest to the window. "It's complicated."

"Fair enough." I shrugged, sitting on the opposite bed. *My* bed, I guess.

"Do you have a boyfriend?" She questioned, wiggling her eyebrows.

I frowned to myself, trying to figure out what the hell was even happening between Archie and I. "No, I don't have a boyfriend." That was the simplest answer I could give.

She nodded slowly. "Well, you'll find one." She sounded confident. Too confident.

"Why's that?" I laughed.

"You look like me." She shot me a smug wink, but she wasn't wrong. We did look weirdly alike.

"Huh," I breathed.

"You know what?" Brooke raised an eyebrow, smiling. "I think you and I are gonna be great friends, Savannah."

I smiled, not quite sure of what to say.

Great friends?

I didn't even know her.

But I needed to *try*.

At least that.

"You sure you're okay with this?" she asked again. "Sharing, I mean. I know it's weird having to suddenly live with strangers."

"Not that weird," I replied with a shrug. "Better than where we came from, anyway."

Her eyes saddened, but she didn't let it last.

Instead of speaking, she pulled a packet of gum from her bedside table and held it out.

"Want one?" she asked.

I blinked. "Uh, sure."

"Sharing gum is basically a friendship contract," she deadpanned. "No take-backs."

I laughed, really laughed, and it startled me how strange it felt in my throat.

"Yeah?"

"Yeah," she confirmed with a nod.

We chewed in silence for a second, then she added, "I know this is a lot. Like, you probably feel like you've landed on another planet."

I nodded slowly, processing her words. "At least it's a really clean, cinnamon smelling one."

That made her grin. "I'm glad it smells like cinnamon and not boys." She scrunched up her nose. "The neighbors are *always* over."

I laughed again. "Definitely smells of cinnamon, don't worry."

"Perfect." Her smile spread wider.

I smiled back, softer now. "I think you're right. I think we're gonna be friends."

I didn't know if it was true. But I wanted it to be. That had to count for something.

TECTONIC

JUNE 25TH 2004

SAVANNAH

"You know you don't have to stay, right?" Liv offered gently, smiling down at me like she knew better.

I hated that question. Not because she was wrong, but because she wasn't. I didn't *have* to be here. But what was the alternative? Go home and sit in a room with my grieving brothers all day? At least here, I could pretend I was someone else—someone whole.

Liv smiled again. Her green eyes were too kind sometimes. Unlike the rest of us, I never caught a flicker of sadness behind them. Liv wholeheartedly believed in the world, and she always had. Sometimes, it was a breath of fresh air. Other times, it was devastating, because I knew the world would turn on her one day.

It was our first day back after the short break, and I'd forced myself to show up despite the way my body begged me to drown in my own bed.

"Most people would be taking weeks off school," Liv continued, tilting her head like she was figuring me out, her curls spilling over her shoulder like something out of a shampoo commercial.

"I'm not one of those people," I answered, voice far steadier than I felt.

"Neither were Theo or Archie." She nodded toward the circle of friends gathered around us. "I'm just saying, you have a choice. A choice to feel your emotions instead of hiding from them."

"I am feeling," I insisted, and it was only a half-lie. I nodded once, begging her to believe me. "I'm not in danger anymore. I'm happy."

She glanced at me, "Your mother…"

"Is dead," I cut her off, pretending those words weren't a knife to the heart. "She's dead, Liv. I can't sit and cry about it."

"Alright," she whispered, leaning back in her chair. "As long as you're okay, Savannah."

I forced a smile, taking a sip of my juicebox that tasted more like regret than sugar.

I should have told my mother I loved her.

I should have let Archie help us earlier.

I should have done a lot of things.

"I'm just fine," I told her, needing people to just *stop* questioning me when I hardly knew how I felt myself.

"Hey there," Josie exclaimed, auburn hair flying in the wind as she slipped into her seat. As usual, her smile was wide, but it didn't quite meet her eyes today. "How are you?"

Before I could muster up another lie, Danny showed up like clockwork. "How are you, Sav?" Same question. Same look. Same pitiful eyes.

Sigh.

"I'm good." I smiled, repeating those words for what had to be the fifth time today.

Everyone had this weird belief that losing my parents would destroy my world.

But grief didn't work like math. It didn't add up or cancel out. It splintered. It grew roots in quiet places, then cracked open your ribs when you least expected it.

Losing *Marlee* destroyed my world.

Losing my father began healing it, and losing my mother just... tilted it to the side for a little while.

That was all.

"Sav." That was Archie. He sat beside me, expression even softer than usual. "Hi."

"Hi," I murmured back. I was thankful he wasn't asking questions. He never did. He just sat with me in the dark.

Billy appeared next, moving like he was being chased by something. His jaw was clenched, eyes darting around before locking onto us. "Have any of you seen Iz?" His voice trembled slightly as he spoke, and I heard it no matter how hard he tried to act casual.

Something about the way Billy asked made the hairs on the back of my neck stand up. He was always a little jittery, but this was something else – like he was bracing for a storm he couldn't outrun.

From what I'd seen, Izzie Harris had *always* been a storm. One that Billy never had, and never would, outrun.

"What's wrong with my sister?" Danny's tone was casual, but his body stiffened like a wire.

Despite the silent war between them, Danny still flinched when someone mentioned Izzie like she was breakable. I knew he held resentment towards his sister, and I didn't entirely blame him, but that never erased the love. The love was a*lways* there.

"Nothing," Billy answered quickly. *Too* quickly. He straightened up then, offering Danny a stiff nod before heading in the opposite direction.

"Hm," Josie hummed. "That was strange."

"Strange?" a voice echoed behind us. Theo. He dropped into his seat like gravity had finally caught up to him. "What's strange? You talking about me again?"

Liv rolled her eyes but couldn't suppress a smile. "We're talking about Billy. Contrary to your beliefs, Theodore, not everything is about you."

He frowned. "It's a shame. I have the bone structure for everything to be about me."

Archie chuckled beside me, his laugh low and warm like a secret kept between us. As always, that sound settled something deep in my chest.

I had no idea what was going on between us.

I knew he was trying to give me space or whatever, and maybe I needed it, but I just couldn't figure it out. I had feelings for him, but that was all I knew.

Could I finally allow myself that happiness?

It was just… hard.

He hadn't even asked about my parents since their death. He just stayed. That meant more than any condolences could.

Archie quietly shifted closer to me. Not enough for anyone to notice, but enough for my skin to register the warmth of his arm beside mine. I didn't lean in. I didn't pull away either.

"You okay?" he asked under his breath, eyes on the horizon.

"Define okay," I whispered back.

His gaze flicked toward me, but he didn't press. That was the thing about Archie. He never tried to save me. He just let me bleed in peace.

"Can we be positive today?" Danny groaned from his chair. "I need joy."

He would regret those words in seconds.

Izzie stormed up to the group, eyes sharp and furious, dropping into her seat like the world had wronged her personally. In a way, I suppose it had.

"Izzie," Liv tried with a bright smile. "Good morning to you too."

"Don't speak to me," Izzie muttered beneath her breath.

Liv leaned back in her chair, the look on her face saying, *Well, I should have known.*

Theo perked up. "You good? You're reminding me of my Aunt Kelsey. Oh, she's a heroin addict. She's great."

"Shut the fuck up, Theo."

"No foreplay?" he replied easily. "It's insane how many times I can say those words in a–-"

"God, you're such a–-"

"Guys," Josie interrupted, waving a hand between the two of them. "Let's not. It's hardly ten in the morning."

Danny nodded, glaring at his sister. "Okay. Relax."

"No, no," Theo said, leaning back, eyes still locked on Izzie. "Let her speak."

"You don't wanna hear what I have to say," Izzie shot back, but it sounded more like a warning. And it landed.

"It *didn't* happen like that," Theo told her slowly, hands thrown up helplessly. "It didn't, Izzie. Your version of the story *isn't* right."

I wasn't sure what they were talking about, but I could tell it hit Izzie like a punch.

"No." Her voice trembled. She looked anywhere but at him. "You're lying. You've been lying since I was nine."

Theo's grin finally faded.

I didn't know what they were talking about. I wasn't sure they did either. But whatever it was – it ran deep. Too deep for a schoolyard.

"I'm sure you've got more to say," Theo muttered with a shrug. "So, continue. Give me all your fucking venom."

"Does it look like I have more to say?" Izzie asked, voice laced with said venom. "Of course I do. I *always* do."

"Not having a good day?"

Izzie scoffed. "No. And I'm surprised you picked up on that, considering you were never good at reading emotions."

He blinked. "Okay, ouch."

"You think it's funny, don't you? That you can say anything and get away with it." Her lip curled. "You've always been like this."

"What are we talking about?" Theo asked, genuinely confused for once. "What—what did I do this time, Izzie?"

"You *lied*," she said. Just that. No volume. Just fire.

Theo's voice faltered. "You still believe that?"

"I know what I saw, and I know what I heard," she spat. "You don't get to rewrite *my* memory because it's inconvenient for *you*!"

"Hey," Liv interjected, gently but firmly. "Let's maybe not start World War Three at the lunch table?"

Izzie turned on her so fast it was like she'd forgotten she wasn't alone. "Of course *you'd* say that."

"What does that mean?"

"It means *you* don't get to play peacemaker when you've been *benefiting* from the war since day one."

The table went dead silent. Even Theo stopped breathing.

Liv blinked hard, clearly trying to make sense of her words. "That's not fair—"

"Nothing's fair," Izzie hissed, standing so abruptly her chair screeched. "But at least I'm not pretending."

Josie, thank god, broke the tension "Liv. Joy. Inject it now."

Liv beamed, a flicker of light in the dark. "My brother's back again," she said, effortlessly throwing her curls into a messy bun. "I haven't seen him for months."

Everything went quiet for just a second.

Theo's smile didn't fall, exactly, but it tripped. "Fun."

Izzie went fully silent, dark blue eyes wild and gutted.

"Are you still coming over tonight?" Liv asked, grinning. Those two had been sleeping in the same bed for far too many years, so I'd chosen to ignore it now. "Adam specifically asked for you to come over."

"Me?" Theo raised an eyebrow, clearing his throat. "Why?"

"Well," Liv started. "He wanted you to come over because he missed you, duh. He also asked about Izzie and Savannah, though."

That earned nothing from Izzie, so I decided to speak.

"He did?" I asked, tilting my head. "Wow, it's been ages."

Liv nodded enthusiastically. "So, are you all in?"

I nodded before shaking my head. "Sorry. Brooke wants to go out tonight."

"Tell her to come, silly." Liv giggled. "Plus, I wanna meet her."

I laughed along with her, waving a hand in the air when I saw Brooke by the oval.

"Hey, Savvy!" She exclaimed, arriving at our table. "What's up?"

"Liv wants us to go over there tonight. Her brother's finally home from college," I explained. "Would you wanna come?"

Brooke nodded almost immediately before frowning. "College?"

"Mm hm," I confirmed. "He goes somewhere in America and comes back every few months."

"Cool," Brooke replied. "Well, I'm in."

Liv's grin stretched wider. "Theodore, you're coming, right?"

"I don't…" He frowned, scratching his jaw before nodding. "Ah, I can do that."

"Well, I'll get Billy to make an appearance," Danny announced, sliding out his phone from the pocket of his blazer. "I'm inviting myself, by the way."

"You're all invited." Liv sighed. "As long as you can be civil with Adam. He's really lovely once ya know him."

Izzie stood without a word and walked away.

Theo nodded absently. "I'm a huge Adam enthusiast."

I didn't know what happened between Theo and Izzie when they were seven.

I didn't know what Liv had done to earn that kind of venom, either.

But I did know this: Izzie was breaking. Not cracking. Breaking.

And we were all standing around watching it happen like it was a show we'd seen before. No, it *was* a show we'd seen before. But I'd hoped – so, so, badly – that we'd never watch it again.

Maybe we were all a little broken. But she was bleeding out, and nobody had the guts to get their hands dirty.

Not anymore.

And now?

She didn't have Billy to wipe away the blood.

And I kept telling myself it wasn't my place. That someone closer would step in. But the truth? No one was closer anymore.

No one was close at all.

Brooke looped an arm through mine, eyes twinkling. "Savvy, we have Maths next. Come on."

I groaned, standing up anyway, but not before taking one last glance at Archie.

Yeah, that was a conversation waiting to be had.

DIE YOUR DAUGHTER

JUNE 25TH 2004

ARCHIE

"Archie." Adam nodded, his chin tilted with that same smug confidence I'd always tried to ignore. He gestured to the seat across from him. "Glad you're here. It's been… what, three years?"

I couldn't tell if the confidence was real or just a front he put on to cover up whatever bullshit insecurities he was hiding.

"A long time," I agreed, careful. Like stepping onto thin ice. I sat, but not too close. *Never* too close.

It felt like walking into a trap I hadn't even signed up for. Every nerve in me screamed to bolt, but I was rooted there, frozen in this weird mix of curiosity and caution. The past didn't want to let go, and neither did I.

I'd never thought too much into the guy, but ever since Sav made those comments at Danny's birthday, I couldn't stop thinking about it.

His expression flickered, only for a second. But I caught it. The twitch in his jaw, the almost-flinch. I wasn't that scrawny kid anymore, and maybe that scared him a little.

"Where's your friend?" he asked eventually. His tone sharpened like a knife, and I already knew who he meant.

"Theo," I replied in a mutter.

Adam smirked like the name was a joke. "That's the one. Still thinks he's the smartest guy in the room?"

"Only when he is."

I said it flat. No sarcasm. No heat. Just fact.

Because Theo *was* the smartest person in most rooms. And Adam knew that.

But truthfully? I wanted to bloody punch him.

Before I could say anything else, or quite frankly rip the head off his body, the door flung wide open.

Everybody arrived at once: Theo, Danny, Billy, Sav, and our newest addition, Brooke.

Then there was Izzie.

She wasn't laughing like the rest of them. Wasn't angry, either. She looked… blank. Like someone had turned the volume down on her soul – the one that was usually louder than most.

Her dark blue eyes darted around the room like she was already searching for an escape, darkening slightly when they landed on Adam. She looked at him like he was the nightmare she still hadn't woken up from.

It only took a split-second for her to look away, but the fear never left.

All of them looked scared.

Sav shifted on her feet. Theo looked at anybody but him. Danny – not subtly – glared at him. Even Josie looked awkward. Billy looked homicidal. Other than Brooke, fear radiated all around.

And that was when I knew.

Something had happened.

Something *bad*.

"Hi." Sav's expression softened the moment she spotted me. "You're here. Good." She sounded almost as relieved as I felt.

I grinned, thankfully rising from my perch on the couch. "You look wonderful."

She tilted her head, a small chuckle escaping those very bloody kissable lips. "I'm only wearing a tee shirt and jeans."

"I see that very well," I said. And yeah, I was looking. Sue me.

Sav smiled, gesturing to the girl beside her. Brooke. I'd only met her briefly, but apparently, I hadn't paid enough attention. Because, fuck, they looked similar. "This is Brooke. Officially."

"Officially?" I repeated, smirking at her choice of words. "Well, nice to meet you, Brooke."

Brooke searched me for a moment, almost as if she was deciding whether or not I was deserving of her sister. A flicker of realisation appeared in her eyes.

Then, without warning, she blurted, "You slept with my friend."

My mouth opened. Closed. Tried again. Nothing came out.

She clapped a hand over her face. "God. Sorry. That was crass."

I glanced at Sav. She didn't flinch. Thank God.

Probably because she already knew.

Maybe because she didn't care.

"Archie." Sav's voice softened again once Brooke wandered outside. "We should talk."

The words hit me like a freight train. Talk meant change. And change meant everything.

"Okay," I whispered, nodding without hesitation. There were a million unspoken words between us, and it was killing me. "Nobody's on the front porch."

She smiled, following after me as I cracked the door open, both of us slipping out into the cold.

The rain had calmed down, but it was still windy, so I mentally reminded myself that I was supposed to be doing the whole mature thing.

I slid my jumper over my head and gently placed it in Sav's lap. "It's cold," I stated simply.

"It is," she agreed, shooting me a grateful smile before pulling my hoodie over her head.

And God, she looked good in it. Like it belonged to her. Like *I* did.

"So…" I started, hoping she'd be the one to lead our conversation.

Because when it came to feelings, I was always the guy who froze.

"So," she breathed, gaze slipping down to my lips for just a millisecond before returning to my eyes. That's where they needed to stay in order for me to focus. "We should talk."

"About?"

She sighed, running a small hand down her face. "A million things."

And none of them easy.

"Well, start somewhere."

She hesitated for a moment before whispering, "If you're going to leave…"

"No," I cut her off before she could spiral. "You don't need to finish that sentence, because I'm not going anywhere."

A tiny, barely visible smile played on her lips. "Ever?" she asked, and it almost broke me.

"Ever."

"What if I can't make that same promise?"

My heart ached, but I forced a smile. "What do you mean?"

I needed to know. Needed to understand.

"I am *hurting*, Archie," she admitted, voice barely audible beneath the wind. "I've *been* hurting for a long time, and I just… I don't want to drag you down with me when I fall."

"That's not what you're doing."

She let out a small laugh, clearly finding my words amusing. "That's *exactly* what I'm doing."

"No," I argued, voice firm but gentle. "You're falling, and you're not used to having somebody there to catch you. Let *me* catch you, Sav."

I glanced into her eyes then, wide and aware as ever, and I could have sworn there were tears. I saw it then. The fear, the rage, the sadness, the grief, the guilt, the resentment. They'd all mixed into one storm. The storm in her eyes.

"Sav?" I whispered soothingly, subconsciously sliding her hand into mine. "You can cry. You can talk to me."

She broke into sobs then, a sight that I'd never seen entirely.

I mean, after the death of her parents, there had been tears. Of course there had, and they were devastating, but not like this. No, these cries were those sort of heart-shattering ones that leave you gasping for air.

Without thinking, I wrapped her in my arms, holding her head softly against my chest. "You're doing good," I heard myself whisper, running my fingers through her soft, brown hair. "You're doing really well."

"Marlee's dead," she sobbed against my chest, not bothering to hide the full-body shivers racking through her. "M-Marlee's… dead. And my Mum… s-she's dead too."

My breath caught, and I did the only thing I could. I tightened my grip around her body, grounding her as she shattered in my arms. "I know, baby." I whispered without a thought, and neither of us truly paid attention to my words. "I know," I whispered. "I know."

Her fingers curled around my shirt like she was clinging on it to stay upright. "It's not fair," she whispered weakly. "It's not fair, Archie."

I nodded. "I know, Sav." *Trust me, I know.*

We fell into a comfortable silence for a while, waiting until she calmed down.

"My Mum wasn't bad," Sav said quietly, head still resting on my chest, but her grey eyes were nearly free of that heavy level of grief they'd been full of a few minutes ago. "You know that, right?"

I swallowed hard. "I never said she was bad."
Just thought it...

"Everyone thinks it," she explained, almost as if she could read my mind. "But that's not true. She just... well, she was just a girl who met a boy, and suddenly, her choices... they weren't hers anymore."

The least she could have done was save her fucking children. All five that she knowingly brought into that home.

Instead, I whispered, "I believe you."

"Archie." Her head rested against my shoulder then, and I could feel her long lashes blinking away the tears. "I think some people are good people pretending to be awful, and some are awful people pretending to be good."

I nodded slowly, almost understanding her words.

"Mum wasn't either of those things." She wiped her eyes with the sleeve of the hoodie, never fully lifting her head. "She was good, and she was... God, she was awful. But a person can be both, right?"

I didn't fucking know.

But I had a huge feeling she needed to hear whatever she wanted.

And I had no problem doing that for her.

"A person can be both," I confirmed quietly, even though I probably hadn't comprehended half of her words.

If the girl I was admittedly falling in love with was hurting, and chose me? I wouldn't be complaining.

But I always thought that was just a dream.

Some fairytale where it's one girl, and one boy, and they get their happily ever afters.

But I was coming to learn, not everything was pretend. Some things mattered.

Some *people* mattered more than I ever believed they could.

"You okay, Sav?" I whispered a few minutes later once her tears had slowed.

"Marlee's dead," she whispered with a smile of realisation, almost as if she hadn't allowed herself to say those words without tears until now. "She's been dead for a while."

I understood.

Grief changes timelines.

I knew exactly how fucked up grief was, and for me, there was nothing anyone could have said to change that. I just needed somebody to stay. So, that's exactly what I planned to do.

Whether it took her months or years to heal and let me all the way in, I would be here. Waiting. Staying.

"You're not alone." I heard myself soothe. "I'll always be here."

"I know," she said casually, but I could see the silent gratitude in her grey eyes. "Thanks."

As much as she attempted to hide her grief and sadness behind smiles and jokes, I could see it. I could always see it.

And then I held her again. Not because she needed it.

But because I did.

TO SHATTER A WORLD

JULY 2ND 2004

SAVANNAH

After everything that happened, I should have been brave enough to talk to Archie. To give him more of an explanation, and tell him how I really felt.

But every time I tried, it was like the words were stolen from my mouth, and I was stuck in an endless silence.

At school today, I tried.

To no surprises, I'd ended up rambling something about the weather being lovely, then announced Liv needed me elsewhere.

It was raining. Bloody raining, and 'nice weather' was the best I could come up with.

So, here I was again.

After another day of avoiding my feelings entirely, I was back at the place I was expected to call home.

"Girls." Adele said, a half-smile on her face. Something was off. Her smiles were usually warm and bright, but this one wasn't. This one barely met her eyes.

"Mum?" Brooke replied, dropping her bag to the floor. "What's wrong?"

"Can you sit?" Adele asked, gesturing to the couch. "Your father and I would like to talk to both of you."

"Do you wanna talk to the boys?" I asked her, taking a seat on the couch. "Jay took them to the basketball courts, but I can message him if he needs to be home earlier."

Adele shook her head. "No, just the two of you."

Yeah, this was weird.

But anything was better than where I came from.

So, I said, "Okay."

Jason appeared behind her then, the same strange expression etched onto his face, like he wasn't quite sure if he should speak.

"Okay, you guys are being super weird," Brooke said with a raised eyebrow. "Who died?"

"Brooklyn." Adele narrowed her eyes, shaking her head at her daughter. "Nobody has died, sweetheart. There's just a few things that we... need to tell you."

"Okay," Brooke and I whispered in unison, leaning back into the couch.

Jason took a step closer then, hesitating before saying, "What we say next might confuse you girls, but I need you to know we didn't expect for everything to play out like this."

"Do you wanna get rid of us?" I heard myself ask, instantly worried.

Damn it. They didn't want us anymore.

"No," Jason replied immediately, shaking his head. "We are not getting rid of you."

As if she couldn't wait another second, Adele cut her husband off as he tried to speak. "Take a look at this," she whispered, placing a small photo frame on the table in front of us.

Brooke laughed at the photo. "Hey, it's me when I was a baby." She then raised an eyebrow. "Who's next to me?"

I tilted my head, confused.

But then Brooke looked at me, and suddenly, I wasn't confused.

I shook my head. "Is that…"

"You," Adele confirmed quietly, hopefulness clear in her eyes. "Please, Savannah. Don't run off—"

And I did exactly that.

What the fuck?

I bolted up the stairs, instantly making a beeline for my bedroom. Well, mine and Brooke's.

Who was my sister!

My twin.

I opened the door, slamming it shut just as fast. I needed to think. To process.

They were my parents?

And they got rid of me?

My whole life…

It never had to be that way at all.

The door flung open then, revealing Brooke.

I didn't want to speak to her. I didn't want her anywhere near me.

"Savvy?" She whispered, biting down on her lip.

I didn't say anything, didn't even lift my head.

"Please talk to me," she said, her voice pleading. "I didn't know."

"It doesn't matter," I managed to say, voice barely audible. I lifted my head just slightly, just enough for her to see the tears streaming down my face. I hadn't even realised I started crying.

Brooke frowned. "Are you mad at me?"

I shrugged honestly. "I don't know how I feel, Brooke."

"You're my sister, Sav. My twin," she murmured, but I already knew that. I'd been made well aware sixteen years too late. "We were supposed to grow up together, and—"

"But we didn't!" I cut her off, voice raised slightly. Then, quieter, "We didn't."

"I know." She nodded, expression unreadable. "I know it's not fair. But don't you want to know me as your sister? I've always dreamed about how it would feel to have a sibling."

"Don't. No, you don't get to do that," I said, voice sounding more bitter than ever. "This isn't a fairytale reunion. You had birthday parties with cake and parents who tucked you in once the night was over. I had..." I paused, blowing out a shaky breath. "I had walls. Locks on every door, just in case. I had a version of a childhood that you never would have survived."

She flinched slightly, but then she just looked sad. Devastated. "That's not your fault. That doesn't mean it can't change for you now."

I knew that.

But that couldn't take away the sting.

Nothing could.

"It was all taken from me, don't you see that? *Everything* was taken from me." I sniffled, willing myself not to cry. God, was I close. "And... now, when I look at you, I'm wondering what *I* did wrong. Why you got love and I got violence. So please, don't tell me how we're sisters like that word can change anything for me. I was lied to for my whole life."

"I just want to know you." Brooke whispered softly. "That's all I'm asking for. We were getting so close."

"I can't. Do you know why?"

"Why?"

"Because I spent my whole life building walls high to make sure nobody crashed them down." I paused, because those walls may have fallen already. She didn't need to know that. "You don't get to knock those walls down now because you had some lovely dream about a sister. I can't let people in easily, and especially not the girl who got the life I begged for every night. The life I was supposed to *lead.*"

"I know," she whispered helplessly, and the resigned look in her eyes told me I was misdirecting my anger. I knew I was, but I didn't know what else to do.

"I need... time." I shrugged. "I'll stay somewhere else for a few nights. I need to get my head right."

She nodded, but didn't say another word.

God, I should have given her a chance to speak. To apologise, even though this wasn't her fault.

Instead, I walked out of the house.

I didn't look back. If I had, I might have ran back inside.

Because I wasn't angry at Brooke.

Hell, I was hardly angry at Adele and Jason.

I was angry at the world.

The air outside was colder than I expected, hitting me like a slap to the face. Because I wasn't mean, and the way I treated Brooke? That wasn't me.

But God, I was so confused.

I slid both hands into the pockets of my coat and just walked. I walked aimlessly for a while, but it didn't matter. I couldn't be there. With her.

Still, her words echoed in my ears like a broken record.

I just want to know you.

But I couldn't.

It wasn't fair. Maybe I was too rough on her, or I was projecting, but nothing I said was untrue. It was all real. She did get happiness while I got violence, and I did have to lead a life of sadness.

After a few minutes, I slid my phone out from my pocket. My finger hovered over his name for a moment.

Then, I pressed call.

One ring.

Two.

"Sav?" Archie said, sounding alarmed. "Did something happen?"

"No," I immediately responded, knowing his mind would only be jumping to the worst of conclusions. I couldn't blame him, either. "Not really."

He exhaled a long, relieved breath before saying, "Where are you?"

My eyes darted around, searching for any hint of familiarity, but I found nothing. "I'm not sure," I answered honestly.

"Can I come get you?" he asked, and I could hear ruffling from the other end of the phone, like he was already searching for keys. "I'll find you."

"Okay," I whispered, nodding even though he couldn't see me. "Thank you."

Then he hung up.

The wait wasn't long, but it felt like forever considering the information I'd just found out.

It still didn't feel real.

The abuse, the deaths. It was all complicated enough before, and I hadn't even come to terms with my emotions. But this? God, this made it so much harder.

Then, the familiar, black toyota pulled onto the curb, and something in my chest settled, like my entire body recognised him as somebody safe.

"Hi," I said, my voice barely above a whisper as I climbed into the passenger seat. "Thanks for picking me up."

He nodded instantly. "Anytime."

I was quiet for a while, and he let it happen. I think, for that reason alone, I fell even harder for him. He let me sit in my silence, even if it wasn't a good way of coping. Even if every bone in his body wanted, *needed* to know what was happening in my head.

"They're my parents," I heard myself admit a few minutes later, fiddling with the charm on my necklace. "Adele and Jason. They're... they're my parents."

His green eyes widened, lips parting slightly. "Jesus."

I bit down nervously on my lip. "I know."

"And... how do you feel about that?" He asked, tilting his head to the side. He pulled the car to a stop then, clearly too concerned to drive. "Give me all of it."

I shrugged. "I don't even know." That was the truth. How the hell was I supposed to feel? "I'm angry, I guess. Or sad."

"Because they gave you away?" He asked softly, not missing a beat.

"I guess so." I frowned to myself, finally meeting his gaze. "Or because they didn't choose me. I mean... I had to live in that home my whole life. And for what? I never questioned it, because they were my parents," I laughed, but there was no humour behind it. "But they weren't. Why the hell would they adopt me into that house?"

Archie nodded along, but he didn't speak. He was letting me get it all out without interruptions, I realised.

I blew out a shaky breath, throwing my hands helplessly in the air. "I don't think it's fair."

"It's absolutely not fair," he confirmed quietly, sliding my hand into his. I don't know if he knew, but that hand was the closest thing I'd ever known to home. "But you've been dealt a shitty hand, Sav. That much is clear. What does this change?"

My head snapped up. "Like finding out my whole life was a lie doesn't matter at all?"

His eyes widened, clearly realising what he said. He ran a hand down his face. "That is not what I meant. I mean, what does this change for *you*? I'm not saying it shouldn't change anything, because it will. I want to know what it changes."

"Everything," I muttered. "Everything."

He nodded in understanding. "Why don't you stay at my house tonight? Might be good to get your thoughts straight somewhere else."

I hesitated, tearing my gaze away from him. "I shouldn't."

"Why?"

Because my self control has proven itself to disappear every time I'm around you...

I thought for a moment before shrugging. "Might not be a good idea."

"Christ, Sav." His hand moved to scratch the back of his neck, clearly frustrated. "I'm not gonna try anything, alright? I think I've proven that."

Mia Jade

"You have." I nodded, a weak smile appearing on my face despite the pain. "I'm sorry."

He matched my smile with one of his own. "I know."

"I'll stay at your house," I agreed, rebuckling my seatbelt. "Thanks."

"Of course," he whispered, expression softening entirely. He started the engine up again, letting out a breath that sounded almost painful. "You don't have to talk about it, but you need to know that I'm here if you want to."

"I know," I answered, and it was honest. Somehow, Archie Bennett was the only person I'd ever trusted with my life.

Funny how that happened.

After a ten minute drive in silence, we were pulling into his driveway. I still could barely contain my shock every time I was here. To get up to his house, it took at least three minutes of driving from the first gates. His front yard had hedges surrounding it, containing his two sweet golden retrievers I still hadn't met properly. It was gorgeous, a place that should have contained more joy, more family than it now did.

It should have contained the same happiness I knew it used to.

But that was taken away the moment his father and sister were.

God, that story managed to hurt me more than my own.

"Here we are." Archie nodded towards his house, instantly moving to open my door. "Mum's not home yet. Should be back around two in the morning, but I dunno."

I nodded slowly, taking his hand as I stepped out of his car. "Okay."

"You study law," he stated, thankfully changing the subject. "I get it now. Why you thought it would lead nowhere." He offered me a sad smile. "You never had the chance."

I shrugged, but he was right.

I didn't have the chance.

I didn't have any chances.

Ever.

"You have the chance now." His smile grew, more genuine now. "Plus, my mum has connections if you ever wanted to go through with it."

"I'm sixteen," I offered him a small chuckle. "Why don't we circle back when I'm old enough to even consider these things?"

He smirked. "So, you do plan on keeping me around?"

I sighed, but I was smiling. "I plan on keeping you around."

Archie's grin widened as he tugged on my hand, gently pulling me closer to the front door. "Good answer."

We stepped inside, the faint scent of old wood and flowers wrapping around me like a warm hug.

"It's already seven." He raised an eyebrow as he glared at the clock like it had personally wronged him. "How did that happen?"

I shrugged, placing my bag down beside the door. "Time is a funny thing."

He stared at me for a moment before nodding. "It is."

"Do you want me to sleep on the couch?" I heard myself ask, even though I knew the answer. "I don't wanna kick you out of your bed."

"We've had this very same conversation before." He shook his head. "I think we've come to the conclusion that we can sleep in the same bed without…"

"Yeah," I answered before he could finish that sentence. "Okay."

"Are you hungry?" He asked, and before I could say no, he held up a hand in protest. "I mean, should we get dinner?"

I bit down nervously on my lip. It still felt wrong allowing him to pay for food when I knew I couldn't pay him back. "I'm not too hungry."

He searched my eyes for a moment, green eyes seeing right through me. "Do you like pizza?"

I released a soft breath. "I do."

His lips curved into a grin. "Let's go get that, huh?"

"Thanks," I whispered, taking a huge bite of my pizza. I hadn't eaten all day, I realised. "I was starving."

"I could tell," he chuckled in amusement, moving to sit at the edge of the clifftop. "It's weird, seeing Ridgewood look so... small."

My head bobbed in agreement. "I know."

He hesitated for a moment before asking, "Do you want to talk about it?"

"I don't know," I admitted, voice barely audible. "I think I need time before I can really be okay with it, though."

"That's fine," he agreed, shrugging. "It's not a small thing. Plus, if it ever gets too much, my door's always open for you."

I smiled to myself, but didn't let him see.

After a short silence, I whispered, "Archie?"

"Yeah, Sav?"

"You're still sticking around," I stated, eyes widening in confusion. No matter how many times he promised to do so, I think a part of me didn't hear it. Didn't want to hear it.

"Of course I am." He lifted a brow. "I told you, Sav. I'm here to stay, no matter how many times I have to say it before you believe me."

"I believe you," I breathed. "I do."

"That very first day," he continued, shaking his head slightly, like he was still trying to make sense of it himself. "That was it."

I frowned. "It?"

He tilted his head, gazing down into my eyes. "Yeah, you."

I bit down nervously on my lip. "Just like that?"

He blew out a long breath, never breaking our gaze. "Just. Like. That."

Neither of us said anything, but his gaze softened more than I thought possible. It was steady and warm, like maybe he'd been holding onto hope just as much as I had.

Archie didn't hesitate this time. He slowly leaned in closer, fingertips resting loosely on my waist, pulling me in just enough.

Our lips finally met. Again. This wasn't a first kiss, it wasn't nervous or confusing. This was a kiss that said, *I know you. I want you. I'm here.*

My hands found their way to the back of his neck, fingers tangling in his hair as the world around us blurred into a quiet nothingness.

He pulled me in closer, chest resting against mine. I expected his heart to be beating in a slow, steady, rhythm, but it wasn't. It was beating rapidly, excitedly. Just like mine.

He deepened the kiss expertly, and I tried not to think about how much more experience he had than me in this area. But, right now? That barely mattered.

He was kissing me.

That was all that mattered.

And he was a bloody good kisser.

When we finally broke apart, neither of us pulled away completely. Our faces were still inches apart, and I felt safer than ever before.

"I'm not going anywhere," he said softly.
And, this time, I knew he was being truthful.
This time, I was certain I belonged here.

SEVEN DAYS

JULY 8TH 2004

ARCHIE

"Just talk to the girl," Billy shrugged carelessly, running a hand through his sweat-drenched hair from training.

He looked calm. Too calm. Like he had his shit together. But I knew better.

Because as long as Izzie Harris existed in the same universe, Billy Hastings would never *truly* have it together.

"Give her clarity," he continued, voice quiet—thoughtful, like he was pulling words from a part of his brain he usually kept locked. "But I think it's already quite fucking clear."

"What's clear?" I lifted a brow, already dreading the answer.

"The way you feel about Savannah," he said, with the kind of certainty that left no room for misinterpretation. No blink. No pause. Just devastating *truth*. "I can see it. Everyone can see it.

And if you or Savannah don't, then you're the only two people on the entire bloody planet this blind."

I groaned and collapsed onto the bench, letting my head fall into my hands.

This gym, this locker room—it was the one place that always left me in control.

Not today.

Because with this girl? There was not one part of the situation *I* was controlling.

"Of course I see it," I mumbled, beyond conflicted.

Because seeing wasn't the same as doing. And doing? That was the hardest part of all.

"Then do something about it," Billy offered like it was easy.

Something about the way he said it made me think that sometimes the simplest advice is the hardest to follow.

"It's not that easy," I replied, shaking my head. "This isn't some normal relationship. Savannah just lost her *entire* family, and her family wasn't exactly good. There's grief and guilt and a million other things. I don't even know what the right version of this looks like."

"I get that," Billy continued thoughtfully. "She has a past that isn't all that lovely, but that had been clear for years. Her past isn't what matters here, and I think she needs you to see past that, even if it's hard."

He paused, looking at me like he was trying to read between the lines I wasn't even saying.

"Sometimes you've gotta look past a *lot* of things."

I laughed. Not because anything was funny, but because the irony was *too* loud, and it was not lost on me. "You and Izzie are not exactly the blueprint for 'looking past.'"

"No," he agreed with a small shake of his head. "We aren't, but we're an example of how things can work despite that." He cleared his throat, realisation hitting him like a truck. "We were."

His voice cracked just enough for me to hear what he didn't say.

This was exactly why I went to Billy when I needed advice that wasn't wrapped in sarcasm or useless banter. Theo would've made it into a joke by now, or changed the subject to something unrelated and stupid. But Billy didn't do that. Billy listened. And more importantly, Billy *understood*.

"What do you suggest I do?" I asked, genuinely interested in what he had to say.

He was the only guy I knew who'd experienced a relationship that was more confusing than it was easy.

"You can have a conversation with her, or you can wait," he said. "But don't wait too long, Cap. You'll break her heart."

My head snapped up. "So I'm supposed to talk to her?"

Talking felt like jumping off a cliff. But maybe, just maybe, it was the leap I needed to take.

Billy sighed, taking a seat next to me. "Her parents only just died. Now, you're the one in this situation, not me. I can't tell you when the right time is. But you'll just know."

I chuckled, but there was no humour behind it. "I don't think I know, or understand anything about this."

"You'll know," he repeated again. "I knew."

"With Izzie?" I asked, even though I already knew the answer.

He flinched slightly at the name, but nodded all the same. "With Izzie. But we're not the best example, you know that."

"There's a 'we' with you two again?"

He sighed like a man twice his age. "I never know. It's like every time we end, I tell myself it's the last time. And then it's not."

"Why keep going?"

"Because I love her," he said, like it was both the easiest and most painful thing in the world. "And because there's stuff none of you know or could understand."

That tracked. None of us *did* understand Izzie. Not fully.

But I always suspected there was more to her sharp edges. She wasn't cruel just to be cruel.

"I don't need to know everything," I started carefully. "But is there a reason she takes that anger out on Theo? Or, at least… does she *believe* she has a reason?"

Billy hesitated. One second too long.

Then he nodded.

And I didn't understand how or why, but I knew it was real.

While Theo could be an absolute idiot, he'd never hurt a fly. Not unless that fly well and truly deserved it.

I honestly doubted there was anything he could have done to Izzie that would explain this endless hostility.

Then again, that wasn't my story to tell, or have an opinion on.

"This is about *you*, yeah?" he said after a pause. "About how badly you need to talk to Savannah before you screw it all up."

Harsh. But fair.

"She knows." I shrugged. "I've told her how I feel, and we both know."

"That's not what I mean, and you know it," Billy chuckled. "If you're willing to wait, tell her that. If you're not? Tell her that."

Of course I was willing to wait.

I hadn't stuck around this long for no reason.

"Alright," I murmured, then my eyes widened slightly. "But she's got that whole thing going on with Adele and Jason…"

Realisation flickered in his eyes. "Right. Maybe give it a week."

"A week," I repeated. "Okay. I can do that."

Seven days.

I could wait.

I could.

"Did you know?" I asked, running a frustrated hand down my face.

It was the question I'd been needing to ask ever since that night—and the question I'd been fearing most.

Because what if they knew?

What if they all knew what she was going through and nobody thought to tell me.

But, Billy answered, "I didn't know." Thinking for a moment, he sighed. "You were up your own ass with basketball back then, but Savannah never hung out with us as kids."

"And nobody thought that was weird?"

"The same way you didn't think anything of it," he muttered in response. "Now? It seems obvious. But back then, it wasn't."

I drew in a sharp breath. "Okay."

Then I walked off.

Because even though Billy was handy for real support—I needed somebody to take my mind away from this girl.

Hanging out with Theo was the perfect distraction—at least in theory.

"Why are your walls blue?" I asked as I flopped down on his single mattress. "I'd put money on the fact they used to be white."

"They were always blue," he replied with his usual grin, stretching out beside me like a cat who owned the place.

I nodded, letting it go. "Why aren't you at Liv's?"

He groaned, throwing his arm over his face. "Her dickhead brother's always there now."

"Fucking creep," I muttered beneath my breath, glancing at my friend. "So, what, he lives there now?"

"Yes," Theo scoffed dramatically. "He acts like *I'm* the one who should leave. Like *I'm* the intruder."

"You are the intruder," I replied without hesitation.

Harsh truth, but maybe exactly what he needed to hear.

He sat up like I'd just slapped him. "I am not. I've been around all this time, he hasn't. If anything, *I* earned a permanent fucking spot. Not him."

"Okay," I withdrew my statement. "I'm getting your drift."

He leaned back again, exhaling. "I could hear him talking about Izzie last night when I was in the backyard. That earned him a punch from Billy."

My eyebrows rose. "What'd he say?"

Theo cleared his throat, affecting a posh British accent despite Adam being very Australian. "*Huh. She's tall now. Or, she's still this mean?*" He shook his head in disgust. "And my personal favourite: *I always knew she was seriously unwell.*"

My jaw dropped. "And he thought Billy *wouldn't* punch him?"

Theo nodded solemnly. "I've said worse. But he doesn't have the right."

"And you do?"

Silence. That rare, weird kind of silence that only ever happened when Theo actually took something seriously.

"Yeah," he finally said. "I do."

"Why?"

He looked at the ceiling, throwing a basketball into the air and catching it again.

"A whole lot of things, Cap. A whole lot of miscommunication."

"That much I gathered. But… what happened?"

He didn't look at me when he said it. "I don't know."

I shook my head, leaning further back on the pillow. When it came to Izzie, I knew it was best not to push. Not to *ask*. Because Izzie Harris was a locked door with Theo holding half the key and refusing to admit it.

Theo changed the subject with an obnoxious grin. "So, how's our girl Savannah?"

I rolled my eyes, suppressing the urge to hit him across the fucking face. "She's not *our* girl, and she's fine."

"Not yours, either," he said, and that one hit too close to home.

I looked away.

Noticing my silence, he blew out a long, dramatic sigh before turning to look at me again. "My dad and I bonded last night."

I narrowed my eyes, entirely aware of his deep hatred towards that man. "You *bonded*?"

"Trauma bonded," he corrected with a proud nod. "He was going on about how I'm the reason he started drinking."

"How is that bonding?"

Theo threw his hands up like it was obvious. "I told him he was one of my biggest reasons to drink as well."

I glared at him.

Then I laughed.

Because no matter how twisted his idea of opening up was, I knew I had a bloody good friend in the guy.

And maybe that was enough—for now, anyway.

But seven days?

Seven days felt like an eternity.

And I wasn't sure my heart could wait that long.

FAMILY LINE

JULY 10TH 2004

SAVANNAH

I'd been hiding in mine and Brooke's shared bathroom for the past hour.

I'd stared at the same piece of cracked glass for what felt like years, trying to organise my thoughts into something manageable. Something that made sense.

But nothing worked.

I couldn't face her. I couldn't face any of them.

God, I could barely face my brothers.

I hadn't spoken to any of them since the reveal. Since the truth came out.

What if they looked at me differently because I wasn't related to them?

I was trying so hard not to cry, but it was nearly impossible when my mind was filled with so many *what if's*.

I didn't even know why I was so angry. I'd never felt rage like this before. Even when my father would—*no*.

That wasn't worth thinking about. Back then, I wasn't angry. Just sad. Or numb. Sometimes hollow. But now?

Now the anger rushed through my veins like a warning. Like a scream.

I *hated* it.

Maybe I wasn't hiding in the bathroom because I was afraid to face them. Maybe that wasn't the reason at all. Maybe I was just afraid of what I might say.

Then, I heard the voice I'd been avoiding most. "Are you okay?" Brooke asked softly.

I wiped underneath my eyes before sliding the door open, but she blocked my attempt at sidestepping her. "I'm wonderful," I said, sarcasm clear in my voice.

God, what the hell was wrong with me?

"You were in there for a while." She frowned. "I just wanted to check—"

I interrupted her by saying, "You always want to check. You're always there! Watching. Waiting for me to magically become the girl you want me to be. Your sister. I'm just not her, Brooke."

She flinched slightly, but quickly regained her composure. "I don't need you to be anyone but you."

"You say that, but every look you give me is filled with hope," I said, shaking my head. "You're waiting for me to be glued back together like it's that simple."

"All I want is for you to let me in," Brooke whispered, clearly hurt. "That's all I'm waiting for."

"I can't do that. So forgive me if I don't feel like unpacking my trauma to the girl who got the life I deserved too." My voice raised slightly, but I couldn't hide the tremble.

"You think I don't ache for you? You think it doesn't kill me just the same?" Brooke said, obviously in disbelief. "Every time I look at you, I feel a crazy amount of guilt, because I see the other half of me bleeding!"

I shook my head. "You don't get to hurt over my pain. My experiences. My life! You didn't live it, Brooke. You weren't the one locked in a room for days at three years old because you spilt a glass of water. You didn't flinch every time you heard a door slam because you knew exactly what came next. You didn't survive that house." I sniffled, tearing my gaze away before she could see. "I did. Stop acting like you were there."

I took a second attempt at walking around her, but once again, she stopped me. "I get it, Savvy. You've been through hell, and maybe I don't deserve to know you," she whispered. "But I'm going to be here when you push me away. I forgive you for shutting me out, for yelling at me. I forgive you for believing you don't deserve to be loved."

I swallowed hard. "Brooke—"

"Please, listen to me. Just this once." Brooke offered me a weak smile. "I know you don't know me very well, and I don't have any right to know you now. "But you've been through a lot, and you've probably pushed away anyone who could help you. I don't know how you handle it all. Truly. Our parents left you, and the man they stuck you with was, without a doubt, the cruelest man in the world and all you want is to love Archie. It's all horrible. But I'm here, I'm trying, and I forgive you for not wanting to know me."

I didn't say anything. I just stared back at her like she was a mirror. This mirror wasn't broken, though. This mirror showed me the girl I could have been.

The girl I could have been was softer, braver. Less broken. Maybe even happy.

"I need to go for a walk," I choked out, turning away. Because that's how it worked. I needed to burn this bridge before it hurt more.

But Brooke's desperate voice stopped me in my tracks. "You don't get to leave."

I froze. "I'm not—"

"You are," she said, taking a step in front of me. "You are always leaving. You're always halfway out the door," she told me sadly. "Maybe not physically. But in here." She pressed a trembling hand to her heart.

I swallowed hard, attempting to hide the lump in my throat.

"You can hate me, you can scream at me, and you can push me away as much as you like," she whispered, voice breaking at the end. "I'll fight for you."

"Why?" I choked out, not bothering to hide my feelings with anger anymore.

"Because nobody else fought for you," she explained. "And I'll be damned if I join them." Her expression softened as she took another step closer. "I'm not letting you leave."

I shook my head, but I couldn't hide the tears welling up in my eyes.

"I can't stop loving you, caring about you just because you push me away," she whispered then.

I swallowed hard, eyes fixed on the door. But I couldn't deny that I somewhat loved Brooke too, because I was still standing here. If she were somebody I truly didn't want to know? I would have left already. "It would be easier if you did."

Brooke gave me a bitter laugh. "Yeah? Well, I don't do easy. Never have." She blew out a shaky breath, tears falling freely now. "Do you think you're the only one who never feels normal?" She asked, tilting her head to the side. "You think I've never looked in the mirror and wondered why I wasn't worth sticking around for? I know I got the life you deserved, but that doesn't mean everything was perfect for me."

That broke something inside of me.

"You'll only get hurt." I felt a tear stream down my cheek before I could stop it. "I seem to ruin everything."

Brooke shook her head like she was begging me to understand. "You don't ruin anything. You survive them." And then, softer, "And I'm not going anywhere."

Without another word, she pulled me into a tight hug. One that, despite all odds, felt like home.

One that should have always been home.

"Do you think the boys are mad at me?" I whispered against her hair.

"Why would they be mad at you?" She pulled away to look into my eyes. "You haven't done anything wrong, Savvy."

I nodded. "I know that, but…"

"You were lied to. I was lied to. They were lied to." She shrugged, smiling slightly. "Nobody will be angry at you simply because you weren't made aware of something that was your birthright to know."

I smiled, because I knew she was right.

"Thanks," I heard myself whisper. "I'm sorry."

"I don't blame you." Her smile spread wider. "But I would really love for you to be my real sister, now."

For a moment, I was silent. Then I rolled my eyes and laughed. "Yeah, yeah. Okay."

"Great." She winked, immediately flopping down on the bed. "So, let's talk about Archie."

This whole sister chat thing felt wrong on a million levels, but I didn't protest. Instead, I laid down beside her. "What's there to talk about?"

"You like him," she stated as if it was the most obvious thing in the world. Maybe it was. "Maybe even more than like." She raised an eyebrow in recognition. "Oh, yeah. You love him."

I sighed heavily, running a hand down my face. "It's… complicated."

"Then let it be complicated," she advised, turning to face me. "Let it be complicated, but don't run away from him."

I smiled and nodded. "I don't plan on it."

She narrowed her eyes. "You promise?"

"I promise."

And I meant it.

For once, I wasn't running.

Not from Brooke.

Not from Archie.

Not from myself.

KISSES AND CASUALTIES
JULY 17TH 2004

SAVANNAH

The music was too loud, the drinks were too strong, and Archie had been silently staring at me since we all arrived at Theo's house an hour ago.

I didn't get it. Why he kept watching me, why he insisted on staying around. But I didn't want to fight it anymore. I couldn't.

I wanted to stop pretending I didn't notice. Pretending I wasn't as tired of this fight as he seemed to be.

There was no point in dancing around it anymore.

I didn't have any more excuses. No abusive fathers to use as a shield.

Sigh...

I'm not sure who suggested the game, but here we were. Our whole group was in a circle in Theo's living room, countless bottles of alcohol I didn't know the name of scattered across the floor.

"I'm starting," Theo announced, cocky as ever, shooting Liv a wink. She tried to hide her blush by taking a long sip of her drink. Theo didn't even notice. Typical.

Liv's fingers trembled slightly as she lifted her glass to her lips, a flicker of something unspoken passing between her and Theo.

Theo chuckled before saying, "Never have I ever kissed somebody I shouldn't have."

Danny immediately raised his glass, as did Josie, followed seconds later by Billy, which earned a scoff from Izzie.

Theo glanced at Danny, then at Josie, then back at Danny. His finger pointed between the two of them, mouth open slightly.

"No," they muttered in unison, answering the question before he had the chance to ask.

Danny chuckled, the alcohol clearly deep in his system now. "Never have I ever... hooked up with somebody in this room."

Josie drank. Izzie drank. Billy drank. Even Danny, who asked the question, drank.

"In this room or in the house?" Theo asked, raising an eyebrow.

Yeah, Theo's parties were never small.

But I liked to block everyone else out.

They weren't important.

Not compared to *us*.

Danny shrugged thoughtfully. "Let's say in the house."

Theo drank without hesitation. Liv looked sideways at him, unamused, then turned her eyes back to her cup. Billy drank again.

"What, more than one person?" Izzie asked, eyebrow raised like she already knew the answer.

Billy sighed. "You know that."

She laughed. A weird, sharp sound that toed the line between humorous and bitter. "Right. That Daisy girl."

"Iz." Billy warned softly, running a frustrated hand down his face.

"I'm good." Izzie shrugged, downing her beer before shooting him a sarcastic wink. "I'm really, really good."

"Anyways," Danny interrupted, shaking his head at the two of them. "Never have I ever been cruel to somebody for no reason."

Nobody drank.

All eyes turned to Izzie.

Theo and Liv looked at her like she was some sort of wild animal, both wide-eyed.

"I *always* have a reason," Izzie retorted easily.

"Wanna share them with us?" Josie asked, calm but genuinely curious. "Because you haven't liked any of us in a long time."

I like most of you," Izzie stated, smiling slightly, but that dropped when she locked eyes with Theo. "And I don't like people that associate with—"

"Iz!" Billy warned, hand gripping hers tightly. His voice dropped low, and he leaned in to whisper something only she could hear. Whatever it was, it worked. Her lips snapped shut.

It wasn't just the whisper that silenced her. It was the way he looked at her. Like they were the only two people in the room. Like her anger was a monster only he knew how to tame.

It had *always* been that way.

Billy's jaw clenched as Izzie's words hit home, but his hand found hers anyway, like a silent apology.

"I'm beginning to think this game isn't the best one for this group of people," Archie murmured beneath his breath, so quiet that only I could hear. "It never ends well."

I didn't say anything, just nodded slowly.

He was right.

"Can we go without this shit for one night?" Danny said, voicing my thoughts and everybody else's. "It's a party, for christ's sake. No need to tear each other apart."

Everybody nodded, mumbling some sort of agreement. Izzie just looked ashamed.

I glanced at Archie, but he wasn't looking at me anymore. He was watching the others, jaw tight, hands gripping his beer bottle with impressive strength. He was as sick of this as I was.

"I'm getting some air," I muttered, slipping away from the group and heading out the back.

It was cooler outside, almost as if the world was giving me a breeze of wind to just let myself *breathe.*

I barely had time to lean against the brick wall before the back door slid open from behind me. I didn't need to look to know who it was.

"Are you okay?" Archie's voice was soft.

"I'm okay," I whispered, then immediately realised who I was talking to. Archie was never somebody I needed to lie to. "I don't know."

His half-smile was gentle. Reassuring. Not pitying. He never pitied me.

"You're gonna be okay," he said, voice sure in a way I wasn't. In a way I hadn't been in a while.

"Yeah?"

"Yeah."

"What's bothering you tonight?" he asked, sipping slowly, giving me all the space I needed.

"I don't like when they fight," I admitted, tucking a loose wave behind my ear.

He nodded. "I know."

There was something about the way he said it. Like he'd grown used to conflict but never stopped hoping for peace.

I didn't say anything, just bit down nervously on my lip and hoped he would either walk away, or speak again.

"It can't be easy." He shrugged, sliding his hand into mine. "And if you want to leave, I'm happy to drive you home."

I hesitated, thinking of the group inside. "I should really stay. Despite the arguments, they're my friends."

His smile stretched a bit wider as he squeezed on my hand. "You're a good friend, Sav. I know they see it, too. They're just too mixed up in their own feelings to appreciate it, sometimes."

This time, I squeezed on his hand – my silent way of thanking him.

After all, his words were the only ones to ever put an end to the loop of thoughts running through my mind.

I probably owed him a whole lot more than "thanks."

"Marlee's been dead for a while." I offered him a weak smile, barely understanding why I couldn't accept that fact. "I just… I keep wondering how much longer it will take them to realise we're all in this together."

"Theo and Izzie?" He asked, raising an eyebrow.

"Them," I confirmed softly. "And everyone else. Nobody's been the same since."

"I don't think anybody's supposed to," Archie offered, speaking from experience. "Grief is one of those things that no matter how hard people try, nobody can make sense of it."

"I know."

"Sav, it'll all work out in the end," he assured me, subtly pulling me closer. I noticed, though. I *always* noticed. "Everyone is still processing it, and it's… it's different for everyone. One day, you'll all be able to make a bit more sense of it."

"I hope so." I heard myself whisper.

"I know so."

I swallowed, letting that sink in."Um, thank you."

His eyes locked with mine. "For?'

"All of it."

His expression softened as he took a more obvious step forward, tucking another loose strand of hair neatly behind my ear. "Don't thank me."

When he tucked that strand of hair behind my ear, it was like he was trying to hold onto something real in a world that kept slipping away

"I'll try," I laughed quietly.

"I'll wait for you," he blurted out. "If that's what you need. I'll wait for you, even if it takes years."

I felt my face soften then. God, he was sweet. Archie Bennett, against all odds, was not the boy I once thought he was. He was *my* boy.

"I'd never ask you to do that for me." I shook my head once

He chuckled, hand lingering on my cheek. "I know you wouldn't."

"Why would you wait for me?" I asked, curious.

He shrugged. "Why wouldn't I? I know what I want. I'm not going to rush you into figuring out what you want."

I stepped forward, balancing slightly on the tips of my toes. "I'm going to kiss you." I immediately regretted my awkward statement, but it was out.

"Okay." He nodded immediately, no hesitation. "You can kiss me."

So, I did.

His hands instantly slid to the back of my neck, careful, like he didn't want to break whatever spell we'd cast over ourselves. I could feel his smile against my lips.

God, I could have stayed there forever.

Deepening the kiss, his hands explored my body, stopping once they landed on my waist.

A few moments later, I pulled back, cheeks flushed to a colour that was probably embarrassing.

I didn't care, though.

Because it was Archie in front of me.

"I don't want to make you wait," I whispered, my forehead still resting against his.

"I know." He smiled, barely visible. "But, maybe it's what you need."

"I want to be with *you*, Archie," I admitted, not bothering to lie. He knew. I knew.

His hand brushed softly against my jaw. "I know. But if you're not ready, that's okay. I'm not going anywhere."

"I won't leave you hanging," I promised him, and I meant it.

In all honesty, I was never going to make him wait.

I wouldn't be able to handle that wait myself.

But it was nice for him to offer.

He smiled again. "I know."

After a few beats of silence, the door slid open. I heard it before I saw her.

Izzie.

I gently let go of Archie's hand, willing him to get the memo. Thankfully, he understood, stepping back and disappearing inside without another word.

Her arms were crossed tight across her chest, but she didn't look angry anymore. She just looked sad. Done. Ashamed.

"Izzie?" I tried, keeping my voice neutral.

"I made Liv cry," she admitted with a sigh, taking a seat on the bench.

My stomach sank. "What happened?"

"I didn't mean to," she added, attempting to act carefree, but I heard the crack in her voice. "I just— she kept going, and I didn't—fuck. I snapped, and now she's upset, and I just…" She glanced up at me, eyes silently pleading with me not to leave. "God, I messed it all up again."

I moved towards her slowly. Carefully. "Why'd you snap, Izzie?"

"She looked…" Izzie glanced up at me, eyes wide and glassy, like she didn't want to cry, but knew she might anyway. "She yelled back, and she looked like him."

"Adam," I whispered, more to myself than her.

"I just don't like him." Izzie turned her head away, hiding the sadness. "I know it's literally not possible for them to look the same, but it happened."

I tried to speak, but she cut me off, almost as if she needed to say this before she lost the words.

"I need to stop, Sav." She dropped her head to her hands, looking defeated. "I can't turn it off."

"What?"

"The anger," she whispered, wiping a hand underneath her eyes. "It doesn't go away." More tears. "I want to be happy, Sav. I want Marlee back, and…" She paused. "I want… I need…"

"Billy," I finished, taking her hand in mine.

"Billy," she confirmed with a solemn smile. "*Always* Billy."

OKAY WAS A PROMISE

JULY 21ST 2004

ARCHIE

"The snow trip was finally confirmed."

That was the first thing Olivia said when she bounced into her seat this morning, cheeks flushed and eyes practically sparkling.

"Isn't that not until August?" Danny asked, sipping his coke thoughtfully.

But Liv just shook her head, a confident little smirk pulling at the corners of her mouth. "It's on the twenty-ninth of July now. Early. Coach changed it. No idea why."

Theo's grin stretched across his whole damn face like it was Christmas morning. "Share a room with me, Livvy?"

Olivia playfully nudged his shoulder before nodding. "Obviously."

I leaned toward Sav, my voice dropping low enough that the rest of the group just faded out like background noise. "That means we share a room. Is that okay?"

She hesitated. Just a flicker. Like she was weighing every possible risk and reward in her head before letting the answer slip out.

"Okay," she replied softly.

Okay. That one word felt like a secret promise between us.

I let out a quiet breath and turned back toward the group, who were already diving into a debate about snow conditions like it was the hottest topic of the decade.

Honestly? I didn't care for snow.

Didn't care for winter.

Didn't care for *rain.*

But if Savannah Grey was there beside me?

I'd freeze every part of me if it meant being near her.

"Is it just overnight?" Billy asked, breaking his vow of silence. He had a weirdly happy-looking Izzie by his side, which immediately set off alarm bells. She hadn't snapped at anyone today. That was either relieving or terrifying.

"Yeah." Josie nodded in confirmation, letting out a dramatic sigh. "Who am I rooming with?"

Izzie raised her hand with a smile that was... unsettlingly genuine. Josie stared at her like she was trying to decode an impossible puzzle before finally nodding.

Josie nodded slowly, as if she was trying to figure out the sudden reason behind Izzie's joyfulness. "Okay then. Cool."

I assumed her and Billy had finally come to a fucking conclusion and that was a weight off her shoulders. Otherwise, she killed somebody and was happy about it.

Either way, it brought a rare peace.

The kind we didn't question when it came. Not around here.

Peace usually meant something was loading in the background. Some next chapter. Some next war.

"Is Coach coming to this one? Danny asked, raising an eyebrow. "He's always there. Like, lurking."

Theo nodded. "Because he's sleeping with the science teacher."

"He's literally married," Josie said flatly, crossing her arms. "With three kids, must I add."

Theo let out a long, suffering breath. "Yeah, well. It was fun to imagine."

Liv jumped in immediately, hands on hips. "You were imagining it?"

Theo's lips parted, then closed. "No," he murmured, barely audible.

"You lot are strange." Billy shook his head in disbelief as if that fact hadn't been clear for a long while. "Anyway, are we taking a bus or what?"

"Two," Josie confirmed with a sad expression on her face. "Coach said it at practice. The first bus is early in the morning by the front gates."

"Define 'early,'" Danny said, narrowing his eyes suspiciously. Yeah, the guy wasn't a morning person.

"Like six-thirty," Josie replied flatly, rolling her eyes. "As in A.M."

Theo dramatically dropped his head onto the table. "Just bury me in the fucking snow when we get there."

"You'll be fine," Olivia said, nudging him again. "I'll bring you coffee. I'll even make sure it has extra caffeine."

"Promise?" Theo peeked up.

"Cross my heart." She grinned, ruffling his hair.

Theo slowly removed her hand like she was holding a bomb. "Hey. Hair like this takes a lot of work."

"You literally jumped out of bed and came to school," Olivia corrected.

"Fine," Theo mumbled. "You're right."

Sav giggled from behind me, and it may have been the most precious bloody noise I'd heard in years. I caught her smile just before it disappeared into something harder to read.

"You excited?" I asked her, low enough that the others couldn't hear.

She shrugged, biting down on her lip. "I think so," she said, eyes meeting mine. "I've never seen snow."

Never?

I blinked. I don't know why that hit like a punch to the ribs, but it did.

She always said things like that. Small. Simple. But they stuck. Like a pebble in your shoe.

"Well," I said, clearing my throat before that pain showed.. "You're gonna hate it."

Her eyes snapped up, wide and fucking beautiful.

"It's cold and wet," I explained. "Maybe you'll hate it. Or maybe, I'll make sure you don't."

Sav's lips twitched for half a second, but I saw it. That almost smile she gave me when everybody else was around, but she was blocking them out.

"Big talk," she muttered, but there was a smile in her voice.

"I'll back it." I shot her a reassuring wink and turned away before I could say something dumb like *I'd set the world on fire if you asked me to.*

Because I would.

And that scared the hell out of me.

I'd kissed her. A few times.

And now? I didn't know if I'd ever be able to stop.

She thought I was waiting to protect *her.*

And maybe, in the beginning, I believed that too.

But the truth?

I was the one terrified.

Terrified of the control she had over me.

Terrified of how badly I wanted her.

Terrified of how *known* I felt when she looked at me.

I knew she wouldn't hurt me, but what if I hurt her? Fuck, that thought made me sick.

She saw straight through me. I didn't even know how much until she stared for half a second too long and I had to look away.

I was completely bloody consumed by the girl, and a mere second without her now felt like torture.

None of it made sense, really.

I'd spent five months falling in love with her.

And it wasn't enough.

It felt like the first few words of a very long book.

A book I wanted to read over and over again.

If she asked, I'd rewrite the ending a hundred times just to keep her in it.

I was in way over my fucking head.

No lifeboat. No goddamn paddle.

Just her.

Yet, I hadn't once thought about swimming to shore.

"What are we actually doing?" Danny asked, clearly confused. "Other than sitting in the snow."

"Coach mentioned skiing," Izzie offered, still suspiciously kind. "But I don't know if it'll happen, 'cause it might rain."

Each of us nodded slowly, careful not to poke the bear.

We didn't need that today.

I sure as hell didn't.

"I am not skiing if it comes to that," I said, dismissive.

"Oh, you'll go," Sav said, looking smug as hell. It was unusual, and I thoroughly enjoyed it. "I'll personally push you down."

I raised an eyebrow at her sudden boldness. "You'd like that, wouldn't you?"

She only grinned, and fuck me, I was so screwed.

But I liked it.

I liked the way she looked at me when nobody else was watching.

I liked the way she could drag me to hell and back and I'd still say thank you.

I liked kissing her. God, I liked kissing her.

And I liked that this trip – this disgusting, snowy trip – had the opportunity to change things.

Whether for better or worse.

I was in.

All. In.

I tilted my head – just enough for her to be the only one to hear. "You sure you'll be okay?" I asked, worry rushing through my body. "You've never come on one of the school trips."

"I was never allowed," she whispered with a shrug.

Fuck.

I figured that would be the case, but I couldn't stand how much she had taken from her. How much I had missed.

"Stop it," she warned, voice soft still.

"Stop what?"

"Thinking," she explained with a small shake of her head. "Worrying. Blaming yourself."

Pausing for a moment, she subtly slid her hand into mine. "Stop all of it."

I blew out a shaky breath. "Okay."

MISTAKE OR FATE?

JULY 29TH 2004

SAVANNAH

The cold slapped me in the face the second we stepped off the bus. Like actual, physical assault. Not the cute snowflakes landing on your eyelashes snow you see in movies.

Those movies were lies.

"This is disgusting," Josie said, clearly regretting her choice of attending.

"I can't feel my ass," Danny added, trailing after Josie and Billy as they approached the cabins.

Olivia? Well, that was another story. She was twirling, actually twirling around in the snow like she'd never seen anything so beautiful. "It's gorgeous. Oh my God."

Theo was recording her with his shitty camera he insisted on bringing. "This is going in the wedding slideshow."

Liv spun as if she was the lead in a musical, and Theo filmed her with that sort of focus you only use when something – *someone* – really matters.

Me? I was trying not to think about the fact that Archie's hand had brushed mine *four times* on the bus, and each time it had felt like my skin was about to burst into flames. Which is ironic, considering we were surrounded by snow.

I liked to think I handled it well. Really, I had. I made jokes and had real conversations with him, and I never made one awkward comment. I didn't even overthink it when our knees touched.

Okay, I did, but only a little bit.

That was progress.

As much as I enjoyed being around him, it was probably good that he decided to give me some space. Some time.

Plus, we did just fine at keeping it platonic when it needed to happen.

Ha.

I could hardly even think that without laughing at myself. There was no way in hell we'd be able to keep it platonic.

It just wasn't how the universe intended for this to work.

Until the moment we stepped foot inside the cabins, everything was great.

Josie looked up from her clipboard, giving me that look. The one I'd never been able to name. But it only ever meant trouble. "Ah, minor issue. We're one bed short."

I blinked hard. "What?"

"Well, they assumed you weren't coming because you never used to," she explained, pointing at her clipboard. "There's only one bed in room three."

My stomach dropped.

She didn't even say it. Just *looked* at *me*.

I turned to him, and despite how sweet he usually was, the bastard was chewing on the inside of his cheek to stop himself from laughing.

God. I loved him.

Shit. I *loved* him.

I swallowed. "Is that okay with you?" I asked, trying to keep my tone casual despite the way my stomach just dropped into my ass. "Sleeping in the same bed?"

It didn't matter that we'd done it before.

It was different this time.

Clearer heads. Clearer lives.

Dangerous decisions.

Archie shrugged like it didn't matter. Like sleeping next to me in the same bed, in a snowy cabin, wouldn't destroy the *already thin* line we'd been toeing for far too long.

He nodded then. "Obviously."

Yeah, that wasn't good.

But I couldn't complain.

Because I did want to be around him.

So, I trailed after him as we headed inside *our* cabin. It was dimly lit with a fireplace in the corner of the small room, candles across the top. It made me more worried than happy, because it felt way too romantic for comfort.

We dumped our bags, claimed beds, pretended we weren't spiraling.

After a few minutes of looking at each other in silence, Liv dragged us all out of our rooms for an 'important snowball fight.'

Look, I wasn't going to complain.

After all, I'd sort of missed out on all of the fun, childish games.

Whether it was to reclaim my childhood or avoid spending too much time alone with Archie, I jumped at the chance.

Ten minutes in, Theo had already ended up on the floor after Liv tackled him. Josie shouted at Danny for aiming too close to her hair, and Izzie was grinning at the mere sight of snow. The sight of Theo chuckling? Yeah, not so much.

And Archie?

Archie hit me once before bolting, because he saw it too. The way every bit of awkwardness I had faded the moment he was around.

So, I chased after him.

"Coward!" I laughed softly, almost reaching him.

"Sorry," he called over his shoulder, trying his hardest not to grin. "I didn't mean to."

I caught him by the sleeve, slipped, and we both ended up in the snow, breathless and freezing and way too close.

For a second, neither of us moved.

It felt like the whole world was holding its breath.

My gloved hand was on his chest. His laugh faded.

"Hi," he said, voice low.

"Hi," I replied, trying not to panic.

Then Josie screamed something about frostbite and shots, and we all trudged back inside.

The drinking had sped up unusually fast, meaning everybody was in bed by ten.

Archie and I hadn't gotten quite as drunk as the others, but that certainly wasn't to say we were sober.

The moment we stepped foot back into our room, it hit me like a truck.

One bed.

One blanket.

One pillow.

One night with the boy who had occupied my every thought since February. The boy I needed to *stop* kissing before I ruined everything.

But I didn't want to stop.

I wanted to keep him.

I climbed into bed next to him, smiling down at his face. I rested my elbows on the bed, allowing them to hold me up.

He raised an eyebrow, chuckling slightly. "Were you planning to watch me sleep?"

I frowned, asking myself the question. Yeah, *not* sober. "I don't know."

His chuckle grew louder. "Well, unfortunately for you, I'm not tired."

I didn't reply.

I just kept staring into his eyes.

God, those eyes.

They would be the death of me.

I knew they would.

I was trying to control myself. Truly, I was. But every last drop of common sense I may have held, had disappeared now.

So, I did what any girl would do if they were in a room alone with Archie Bennett.

Just with more meaning.

I leaned in close, kissing him without hesitation.

This time, it wasn't soft. It wasn't gentle. It was passionate and rough and a kiss that should not have been happening

I mean, we were both drunk.

But who ever said teenagers were supposed to make good decisions?

Plus, it wasn't like I didn't enjoy kissing him without the alcohol.

I really bloody did.

Maybe the drinks were just the push I needed.

He froze for a moment, like he wasn't sure if this was the right thing to do, but eventually, he gave in, deepening the kiss with skill.

I tried to ignore the fact that his skill had very obviously come from experience. Thankfully, I was too consumed by him to let those thoughts take over. Not tonight.

His hands found my waist, making their way down my body. He shifted, positioning himself to hover above me with a genuine smile despite the questionable situation we'd ended up in.

"Sav," he whispered, voice low and rough around the edges as he gazed into my eyes. "Are you sure? One hundred percent?"

"I've never been more sure of anything," I replied without hesitation, and it was true. I threaded my hands through his hair, pulling him in closer. "Just... be careful."

He smiled lovingly. "Of course."

I didn't care about the consequences. Not tonight. Because I knew, deep down, there was nothing I would regret when it came to this boy.

His mouth was everywhere. My lips, my neck, my collarbone, but it wasn't enough. I needed more.

It was a strange feeling, because this had never happened before.

Then again, I'd never felt any of these things until Archie Bennett walked into my life and completely flipped it upside down.

Archie groaned, low and deep, and I felt it more than I heard it, vibrating against my skin. He pulled back just far enough to look down at me. "Sav. Talk to me. I need to know that you're very, very fucking sure."

I nodded rapidly. "I'm sure, Archie."

Clothes became a problem we were suddenly very motivated to solve.

His shirt was the first to go, tossed somewhere I'd definitely forgotten. God, that first day, I didn't think the boy could get any more attractive. Tonight, I knew that thought was wrong.

Then, he glanced down at my shirt.

His eyes locked with mine, asking me a silent question that I had no problem answering. I nodded, lifting my arms above my head.

With a shaky breath, he slowly slid my shirt over my arms.

"We're not having sex tonight," he informed me, hands resting on my hips. "But we can do other stuff. If you want."

I nodded eagerly, happy to take anything he'd give me.

For a moment, we just stared at each other. No words, no moving.

And it was perfect.

Until he said, "I can't, Sav." He dropped his head to my chest, exhaling a ragged breath.

I frowned, disappointed as much as I was humiliated. "What do you mean? Did I do something wrong?"

"No," he was quick to clarify. He moved his face closer, gently resting his forehead against mine. "God, no. You did everything right."

"So… why did you stop?" I asked, more confused now. "Do you not want to?"

"I can't do that to you," he admitted, but his voice wasn't even a whisper. It was more like a breath. "I know you said yes, and I… fuck." He ran a hand down his face, clearly conflicted. "Of course I want to. But I'm not taking anything away from you on a school trip. Especially one where we're drunk."

I frowned, not speaking.

A weak chuckle managed to escape his lips. "Look, before I met you, I was…"

"A bit of a man-whore?" I asked softly, hardly even realising my words as they slipped out.

His chuckle returned at my bluntness. "Yeah. Probably. But the point is, I don't care about that now. You're… *you*."

"Is that a bad thing?" I asked, suddenly self-conscious as I slid my shirt back on.

"Absolutely fucking not," he assured me, flopping down on the bed beside me. "It is a wonderful thing. Something that I can't risk ruining for *this*." He vaguely gestured around.

"But you were doing lots of things with other girls." I frowned, searching his eyes. Tangling his hair in my hands, I whispered, "I don't want you to stop spending time with me, or walk away from me, because of this."

His head snapped up. "That is not what's happening. I'm saying no because I don't want to leave you with any regrets." He smiled, tenderly rubbing his finger across my cheek. "I want it to be perfect for you. Everything we do. I want it all to be perfect."

I managed a smile, glad that this wasn't his super-secret plan of getting rid of me.

I blew out a sigh of relief. "Okay then."

"Yeah?" He nodded along, sliding his hand into mine. "I promise, you'll feel better. You're drunk right now, and so am I. No matter how badly I want you, which I do, I can't hurt you like that. You'd regret it so badly in the morning."

"Okay," I whispered, smiling at his respectfulness. Maybe he was right, anyway. "Well... thank you."

"Of course," he answered. "Now, are ya good to sleep in a bed with me or do I need to sleep on the floor?" he teased, nudging my knee.

I giggled, laying back down against my pillow. "I can sleep in a bed with you, Archie. We've done that before."

"Okay," he said, purposely emphasising the Y. He squeezed on my hand, letting his eyes flutter closed. "Good night, Sav."

I smiled, allowing mine to do the same as I rested my head closer to his. "Good night, Archie."

I woke up to the faint crackle of the dying fireplace and the noise of somebody ruffling in the next room. For a moment, I couldn't figure out why I was so warm. Maybe something went wrong with the fireplace.

But then, I realised I wasn't alone.

Archie's arm was draped over my waist, his breathing slow and steady against my back. He was still asleep, no movement other than the rise and fall of his breathing. He looked... peaceful.

More peaceful than I'd ever seen him.

Ah. Forgot about that.

I should have moved. Rolled over, created space. But I didn't.

I stayed.

I closed my eyes for a moment longer, allowing my mind to drift away to the thoughts of last night.

The kiss.

The way he looked at me like I was something rare. Something worth more than I'd been given.

The way he said no, not because he didn't want me, but because he respected me.

God, he *respected* me.

I wasn't quite sure what to do with that.

I mean, I never doubted that he had a lot of respect and care for me, but at the end of the day, he was still a boy. A boy that didn't exactly have the best history when it came to sex.

But he didn't force me. He didn't make me feel like I needed to do that for him to stick around.

That meant more than he could ever realise.

So, I stayed still. I inhaled the faint scent of the vanilla candle mixing with the burning firewood, allowing myself to feel a new sense of peace.

Maybe I did deserve peace.

Eventually, Archie stirred beside me. He let out a sleepy breath before tightening his grip on me ever so slightly. "Are you awake?" he whispered softly, like maybe he wasn't sure if I wanted to talk this morning.

I nodded, not trusting myself to speak just yet.

He didn't let go. In fact, I was sure he scooted closer to me. "You alright, Sav?"

"Yeah," I said softly, less worried about what I might say. "You?"

He hummed, head resting against the back of my neck. "I am now."

None of us said anything for a few minutes after that.

Maybe it was bad form not to communicate after the night we had, but I don't think it mattered. It felt strangely normal, laying in bed with him, ignoring the rest of the world until it forced us to wake up.

Then again, he always had a way of making me feel at home, even when I'd been worried about letting him all the way in.

Despite my best efforts, I realised that happened a long while ago.

He was in.

So. In.

And so was I.

After a few minutes, I turned to face him without thinking.

His hair was a mess, brown strands sticking up in forty directions, and his eyes were half-lidded like he wasn't quite ready to leave this moment. Somehow, even like this, he still looked perfect. And he still looked at me the same way that had caused me to fall for him.

"Do you still feel the same?" I forced myself to ask, knowing the outcome would be worse if I didn't. My heart was pounding rapidly to the point I could hear it in my ears, but I couldn't let that matter. I needed to force myself to speak before I broke.

"About not sleeping with you?" he asked, voice lighter as he raised an eyebrow. "Yeah. I'd do the same thing all over again."

I scoffed quietly, tucking a flyway strand behind my ear. "No. About *me*."

He pulled his head back slightly like he couldn't believe I was asking that question. "About you?" he repeated, chuckling softly. "Savannah Grey, I have had the same opinion on you for a long time now. I've been sold since day one."

I smiled at his words, but belief didn't erase the lingering fear. I think there had been a million *what ifs* living in the back of my mind since the moment I realised I wanted him. Because it was terrifying. Especially for a girl like me.

Still, he was all I wanted. And I knew, deep down, that he could love me right. But I didn't want him feeling like he needed to love my pieces back together.

"What happens now?" I asked, voice barely above a whisper. That was the one question I *needed* an answer too. Maybe he'd done these things, but I sure as hell hadn't.

He sat up slowly, resting his head on his elbows so he could look at me properly. "We take it slow. We talk. We don't pretend it never happened, but we don't rush things either."

"Slow," I repeated, more to myself than him. "Are you sure you can do slow?"

He smirked. "For you? Yeah. I can do slow. I can do anything. Even if it kills me."

I laughed, the knot in my chest finally starting to loosen.

Someone banged on the door then, causing both of us to jump.

"The bus is in an hour," Josie called from the other side of the door, not opening it. "Breakfast is ready if you're hungry."

Footsteps. Then, silence.

Archie groaned. "I don't think she slept."

"Josie never sleeps," I replied, smiling at the memories of each night she kept the rest of us awake. "Come on, we better get out there or they'll all assume we had sex."

He laughed in response, reaching for his shirt that he discarded in the corner of the room. "To be fair, we did, *almost.*"

"Almost doesn't count."

He grabbed my wrist before I could stand, his grip loose and gentle, yet tight enough to make me focus. His eyes were suddenly serious. "Hey, I meant everything I said. We're okay?"

I looked at him. At the boy who felt like home and a battlefield all at once. Nodding, I said, "We're okay."

Then, before I could lose my nerve, I kissed his cheek, quick and light, and stood up. "Now, I need some coffee."

DON'T BE ME

AUGUST 1ST 2004

SAVANNAH

I barely had time to open my eyes this morning
before I heard the chaos unraveling downstairs.

But it wasn't the usual, angry chaos I was used to.
No, it was laughter and music playing softly in the
background.

I was still adjusting to an, and I was having a very
hard time doing that. While it must have been hard
for everyone, my circumstances were very different.

I wasn't sure how to adjust to this life when it
turned out it was the life I should have had from day
one.

I hadn't really spoken to Adele or Jason. I hadn't
asked them questions or told them I forgave them.
Maybe it was impossible to forgive them until I knew
why they gave me up. Why I wasn't good enough.

But I had to be brave this time.

Because my brothers felt safe enough to live now.
Leo didn't hide in his room with Aidan, Malcolm's

fists didn't clench whenever somebody spoke, and even Jayden was figuring it out quicker than me.

So, I forced myself out of bed despite the way my legs were threatening to give out.

I had to face them some time. It may as well have been today.

When I arrived at the bottom of the stairs, I paused at the sight of everybody baking pancakes in the kitchen like it was the easiest thing in the world.

God, why couldn't I let it all go that easily?

I dragged my feet along the floorboards, finally making my way to the kitchen. My eyes locked with Brooke's first, who was smiling at me like she'd known me for years. I matched her smile with one of my own.

Despite my anger in the beginning, none of this was her fault. Maybe I got the short end of the stick, but that wasn't Brooke's choice.

Plus, she was my sister.

I always wanted one of those.

"Pancakes," I stated, smiling as I joined Malcolm by the bench. "Maple syrup?"

"You know it." He shot me a wink, swirling the whisk in slow, sturdy movements. "Do ya want some?"

"Of course, bud." I nodded, willing myself to stay strong.

I glanced back over to Brooke, who now had Aidan resting on her hip. He closed his eyes, head relaxing on her shoulder. God, even Aidan knew this was how family was supposed to be.

Jayden was chatting with Jason by the back patio now, and even he looked happier than ever. Jayden never showed emotions. Never *used* to.

Leo spilt milk all over the bench now, causing a small chuckle to escape my lips. Jason, my apparent *father*, caught it immediately.

"What's so funny?" he asked, now standing in front of me with a smirk.

"Nothing," I said, then smiled. "It's just... nice, I guess."

His smirk turned into a genuine grin. "That's a new word from you. I'll take it."

I laughed softly as he made his way back over to Jayden, my eyes returning to the kitchen.

Brooke quickly made a beeline upstairs, and for whatever reason, I felt the need to follow after her. I never thought I'd say it, but I needed sisterly advice.

"Brooke," I whispered once she exited Aidan's room. "I need help."

Her eyes widened slightly before she gestured for me to follow her into our bedroom. "What happened?"

"Something happened on the snow trip," I blurted out.

"With Archie?" She smirked, clapping her hands together. "Tell me everything."

I scoffed in disbelief. "How do people *know* these things?"

"Because I've seen the way he looks at you, and I've seen the way you look at him," she explained happily. "That's not platonic, and it's certainly not casual. Continue."

I sighed, resting my head on the pillow. "Okay."

So, I explained everything to her. Every detail that still hadn't left my mind since that night.

It was all on a constant replay.

Once I finished, her face said it all. I think she had more feelings about it than I did.

"I don't even know what it meant," I muttered honestly, shrugging one shoulder. "It obviously wasn't nothing."

"So it meant something?" Brooke asked, but her smile told me she already knew the answer.

"Yeah," I breathed. "That's why it's scary."

"Of course it's scary," Brooke offered, speaking with her hands. "Because you've fallen for him."

"Have I?" I raised an eyebrow, completely uneducated on the topic.

"Yeah," she confirmed with a rapid nod. "You've fallen for him."

I bit down on my lip. "What do I do?"

Brooke thought for a moment, then I could practically see ideas flying through her mind. "You should talk to Jayden."

"About relationship things?" I immediately giggled. "What good would that do? He hates the idea of me dating."

Brooke rolled her eyes, laughing along with me. "Yeah, but he's the only one who understands growing up the way you did, and still finding love outside of that."

"You're right," I whispered, nodding with determination. "I'm gonna do that. Thanks, Brooke."

As I left the room, I glanced back once. She was already curled up on her bed, scrolling through her phone. Like nothing monumental had just happened. But something had. Something huge.

I'd told someone. I'd said the thing out loud.

And maybe the moment you say something aloud, it stops haunting you and starts becoming real.

Once I arrived downstairs for the second time today, I could already see Jayden outside. He was shooting a basketball through the brand new hoop, never missing a shot.

I sat down on the edge of the bench, wrapping my arms around my knees. I didn't say anything. Not yet. I waited, hoping he'd look over. Acknowledge me. Do anything to make this conversation feel less terrifying.

He didn't.

Of course he didn't.

Jayden only acknowledged things when he was forced to. It was his favourite form of power. Like if he ignored the world long enough, it'd forget about him.

So I blurted, "Wanna hear something awful?"

He caught the ball mid-bounce and rested it against his hip, finally glancing over with a sigh. "Is it about you and Archie Bennett?"

I gasped, clutching my chest like he'd just accused me of murder. "Is everyone in this house a bloody psychic?"

He chuckled, dropping the ball to the ground and offering me his full attention. "No. You're just obvious."

Jayden shrugged, tossed the ball aside, and walked over like he had all the time in the world. He dropped down next to me and stretched his legs out, his knee bumping mine. He didn't say anything right away, which usually meant he *was* going to say something important. Eventually.

I blew out a shaky breath and whispered, "I think I'm scared of what it *could* be, because what if it all ends badly?"

Jayden shrugged. "But what if it doesn't?"

That answer took me by shock.

Especially from Jayden.

He wasn't positive.

"You don't get it." I heard myself groan, even though he may have been the only person in the world who did get it.

"I get it more than you think," he offered. "I've seen you flinch when good things happen. I've *been* the one flinching when good things happen."

"But in our experience, good things don't last." I frown. "And this is really, *really* good, Jay."

He smiled slightly. "That's why you hold onto it harder."

I tilted my head, suddenly extra thankful for my brother. "You're really giving me relationship advice? You've always been pretty against me with boys."

"No, I've been against you and sex," he corrected, looking disgusted. "I *am* against you and sex."

I laughed softly, causing his brown eyes to widen. "Did you have sex with him?"

"God." My laugh loudened as I nudged his shoulder. Then, I was suddenly serious. "I think we got close."

Jayden groaned and shoved his hands over his ears. "Don't say *close,* Jesus."

I let out a long, dramatic breath. "Who else can I talk to about sex?"

He rubbed the back of his neck, still obviously uncomfortable but not running away. That had to count for something.

"Literally *anybody* else."

I nodded. "When is Caroline coming over?"

He immediately scoffed, shaking his head slowly. "*Anybody* but Caroline. Christ, *not* Caroline."

I laughed at his reaction. "Fine."

"Don't rush it," he told me, squeezing his eyes closed like he was wishing himself away from this conversation. "Seriously, you've done pretty fucking well compared to the other girls in your grade."

I narrowed my eyes. "And you want me to stay like that forever?"

"I want to *never* have this conversation again," he snapped, voice full of fake outrage. "And I want you to talk to literally anyone else about the word 'sex.' Go journal. Talk to your pillow."

"You're being ridiculous."

He clutched his chest. "*I'm* being traumatized."

I laughed again, leaning forward to rest my arms on my knees. "When is Izzie coming over?"

He eyed me warily. "Why?"

"She's had sex, hasn't she?"

Jayden let out this wild, hyena-level laugh that made me jump. "It's Izzie, Savannah. She probably had sex *at* church camp."

I eyed him. "That's mean."

"No," he said, still grinning. "It's accurate. And I'd still rather you talk to her than me. You'll always be the baby in my eyes."

"I'm not even two years younger than you," I informed him. "You were doing… well, stuff way younger than me."

"Don't be me," Jayden said without hesitation. "Be you. Be *better*."

I nodded slowly.

That stuck with me. Even after he stood up and glanced at his watch.

"Alright, kid. I've got practice."

"Bye." I smiled, waving him off.

My phone buzzed in my pocket, causing me to immediately reach for it.

Archie: Just checking in. You okay?

I didn't respond right away. I just stared.

Then I finally typed:

Savannah: I think so.

Archie: Then that's enough for now.

I smiled to myself, sliding it back into my pocket.

Maybe it wasn't about choosing between old and new anymore. Maybe I could grieve and find happiness at the same time. Maybe it was about building something better out of both.

It was late at night when the house fell into silence. It wasn't uncomfortable. It was peaceful. For the first time in a while, I wasn't aching to be somewhere else.

I sat cross-legged on the edge of Aidan's bed, watching as he slept. I smiled at the way he no longer looked scared in sleep.

"Hey."

I turned to find Leo standing in the hallway, hovering as if he wasn't sure if he was welcome inside. "Can I come in?" he added.

"This is your room." I laughed softly, moving to his bed and patting the spot beside me. "He's been asleep for a while."

His smile was soft as he joined me on the bed. "Jayden said you talked to Brooke."

I nodded happily. "Yeah. I shouldn't have gotten angry at her."

Leo shrugged, almost as if he understood. "Well, Savvy, you were the last one of us to misdirect our anger. Other than Aidan, I guess. Although, he did scare me sometimes."

I chuckled at his absurdity.

Leaning back against the wall, Leo shot me a look. "I used to imagine the house was a spaceship."

I frowned. "What?"

He chuckled softly. "Back at the house. When I was a bit older than Aidan, I liked to think of it as a spaceship. It helped to block out the noises."

I sat up a little straighter, watching him intently. "That's this house," I told him. "We just had to grow up a little wrong."

He met my eyes with a smile. "Only a little."

"We're good now, Leo," I soothed with a smile, finally realising it myself. "We're safe."

"Hell yeah we are."

SHE GOT AWAY

AUGUST 10TH 2004

ARCHIE

Sav was doing it again. Smiling like everything was fine. Like nothing had *ever* been wrong.

And I knew. I knew I was supposed to be ecstatic about the fact she finally got away, that she got to find herself again.

But it was easier said than done.

She hadn't said a bloody word. Her father, her *abuser*, died. Her *mother* died.

Fuck, I knew they were entirely different circumstances, but even I wouldn't have been able to keep myself together this well after the death of dad and Elsie.

And back then, I was a total fucking prick. Showing emotions wasn't my thing. But in a situation like that? You don't have a choice.

At least, that's what I thought.

Christ, I was happy for her. I was so damn happy that she lived. She got to be happy. To grow up.

But she needed to talk about it before it took control over every aspect of her life.

The girl sitting across from me was a perfect example of what can happen if you keep everything bottled up for too long. Izzie wasn't always this way. She was always a bit off, a bit different, sure, but she wasn't angry. She was truly a sweet girl.

But she let her emotions get the best of her.

I just couldn't fucking stand to watch that happen to Sav. Especially now.

I just wasn't sure what I was supposed to do. What I was allowed to do, considering I had no business involving myself here when, chances were, I still needed to prove myself to the girl.

But I cared about her.

I cared about her too damn much to let her fall into that hole. The one you can't get out of regardless of how many ropes get thrown for you.

I just wanted her to be okay.

Fuck that, I needed her to be okay.

When I finally glanced up from the stand of our lunch table, the first thing I noticed was Izzie throwing mental daggers at my friend.

Well, the first thing I noticed was Sav.

But the second thing I noticed was the fucking emotional war going on at our table. One that nobody else seemed to have picked up on yet.

I think Olivia noticed it then, though, because her eyes widened slightly before she glanced between the two of them not-so subtly.

"I got a job," Olivia beamed, offering all of us a way out before another full-blown argument started. She wiggled her eyebrows and added, "I'm a cafe star."

"Star?" Izzie raised an eyebrow. "Are we five years old?"

Olivia frowned. "No, I'm excited."

Sav smiled at them both from beside me, saying, "I'm proud of you, Liv. That's great news."

Always the savior.

"Eleanor's cafe," Olivia explained, focusing on Sav and avoiding Izzie's harsh glare.

"Caroline's mum?" Sav asked with a smile, tilting her head to the side. "That's awesome, Liv. I always wanted a job there."

"Get one!" Liv exclaimed, a grin stretching across her face. "We can be work buddies."

"I can't, he--" Sav paused, realising her next words weren't valid anymore. She smiled slightly to herself, as if she'd just come to the epiphany of safety. "I'll talk to Care next time she's over."

Liv giggled softly, nodding. "Please do. It'll be so much better with you around." Then she frowned. "Adam didn't work 'till he was seventeen, but mum's been on my back about it since the moment I turned fifteen."

"Adopted privilege," Izzie snickered, causing Billy to drop his head in his hands.

"Izzie," Sav warned, eyes widening. "Don't be mean."

Sav had a bad feeling about Adam, but Olivia had been her friend for what sounded like a million years. It made sense why she defended him, I suppose. But I couldn't help her with this one. I wasn't a fan of the guy.

"Izzie." Olivia frowned. "Why don't you like Adam? He's always been super nice to you."

Izzie rolled her eyes, but Billy's hand sliding over hers caused her to pipe down. Whatever she was preparing to say, we didn't need it. Not today.

Still, she scanned Theo once-over, looking anything but amused.

"Is she medicated?" Theo asked, sounding genuinely curious.

"Oh, fuck off," Izzie fired back, narrowing her eyes. "You don't have the right to speak to me that way."

"But you have the right to speak to *me* that way?" Theo asked, clearly in disbelief. "Fucking double standards."

"Not double standards," Izzie argued, but her voice broke off at the end. "Morals."

"Morals," Theo snickered, breaking into laughter. Like, head thrown back laughter. Yeah, he wasn't doing well on the Izzie-metre today.

"If you really want to go there, we can—"

"Iz!" Billy snapped, wrapping a protective arm around her waist. "Please don't start this bullshit today."

"Bullshit?" Izzie repeated, immediately rising from her chair and flipping him off. "You're as much of a coward as he is."

"Iz, don't—"

Then she stormed off.

Of course, Billy followed without hesitation.

He always followed.

For a moment, the table fell into an awkward silence. Then Theo muttered, "Jesus. That girl's a ticking time bomb."

"Don't," Sav said softly but firmly.

I placed a hand over hers, catching her attention.

"Can we talk?" I asked gently, leaning in.

"Is it bad?" she whispered back.

I chuckled slightly before shaking my head. "Not bad. Come on."

By the time we reached one of the empty classrooms, Sav was searching my eyes like she was looking for an answer before I even asked the question.

"Calm down," I soothed, smiling at her. "I'm not here to yell at ya, Sav."

Her body visibly untensed as she joined me by the back. "Are you okay?"

"I am." I nodded in confirmation, looking into her grey eyes. The ones that, despite everything, never quite got rid of that lonesome look. "You're not."

"I am," she defended, but it was weak. "I think I am."

"You have to talk about it," I whispered, smiling sadly. "You can't keep it all bottled up."

"I don't need to speak about it."

"Sav, you can't brush it off like that," I spat out, eyes locked on hers. "You've been through hell. I need to know that you see that. You are allowed to be hurt. You're allowed to be angry, or sad. You're allowed to feel whatever you want because these aren't normal circumstances."

She blew out a shaky breath, finally nodding. "I was hurt. And maybe I was angry. But Archie, it was so long ago."

I shook my head, but I understood. Despite the fact that her parents hadn't died all that long ago, she'd been living in the middle of this horror for her whole life. I couldn't even begin to imagine it.

"I know it was a long time ago for you, but that doesn't make it any less painful. Trauma doesn't have an expiration date," I offered. "It stays with you. It… it does. No matter how much time passes, you're still allowed to feel anything you feel. In fact, I'd be more worried if you *weren't* hurt and angry. I am worried."

Her expression softened. "You don't need to worry about me, Archie."

"Apparently, I do," I said, voice just above a whisper. "I've been worried since the day I met you."

She flinched at my words, turning away slightly. "I'm sorry."

I reached out, gently catching her wrist with my hand. "Don't do that. Don't, because I've also been okay since the day I met you."

"Yeah?"

"Yeah," I confirmed quietly, only just coming to the realisation myself. "Yeah."

"He was never good," she blurted out. "My father, I mean. When I was little, he had a few good days. But if I had to be honest, my best memory of him was…" She hiccuped a sob. "The day he died."

I swallowed hard. "And…" I whispered, fighting back my own tears now. "And your mother?"

"She loved us," Sav confirmed, gazing out of the classroom window. "But she was too weak. We couldn't save her."

"But you loved her?" I asked.

"Sometimes," she said weakly. "I would have never survived in that house, Archie," she informed me, voice cracking. "I always knew we wouldn't all make it out alive. I just… I guess I never thought my mother would be the one to die."

I nodded slowly, still not speaking.

I'd learnt not to when I got her opening up.

It was rare, but when it happened, she needed silence. She needed room.

"My dad was an awful man." Sav shrugged, blowing out a long breath. "But my Mum wasn't terrible. She was just…" she dropped her head to her hands, clearly speechless. "She never had the chance to be good."

I sniffled, tilting my head backwards just enough to stop the tears from flowing.

Sav didn't stop. "I don't blame her, and I could never hate her. But we just… we couldn't save her, Archie."

"You weren't born into a family that taught you love," I offered softly, feeling the need to speak now. "I know, Sav. I know you loved your Mum, and I can't tell you how fucking sorry I am that this happened. But don't let that take away the bad. You need to... you need to allow yourself to feel."

Sav nodded, smiling slightly through the ache. "I know that."

"You're doing good," I told her, rubbing a hand gently up and down her upper back. "You're doing really bloody good."

"Thank you."

"We're gonna be just fine. You're gonna be just fine, huh?"

She finally lifted her head. "Yeah."

"Come here," I whispered, wrapping my arms around her. "I'll never let anybody hurt you again, do you hear me?"

She smiled up at me. "I hear you."

MONSTERS NEVER DIE

AUGUST 13TH 2004

SAVANNAH

"Seriously, Liv, you have enough pillows to sink a small boat." Josie announced as we all stepped into the familiar comfort of Liv's bedroom.

"A cruise ship," I corrected with a laugh.

Liv shrugged, all sunshine and pride. "Comfort is king."

"So, what's the plan?" I asked, flopping onto her bed. And, God, I always wondered how somebody could have such a perfect mattress. It was like sitting on a cloud.

"We watch movies and eat ice cream," Liv explained casually. "What else?"

Josie chuckled as she pulled out a sleeve of Oreos. "I like you, Liv."

Liv scrunched her nose, like she wasn't sure whether that was an insult or a compliment. "I sure hope so."

I smiled, but my eyes drifted to the bay window, to the rug where Izzie sat cross-legged. Her hoodie sleeves were pulled over her hands, and she was absently tugging at the hem like it held answers she couldn't say out loud. Quiet, withdrawn – but still here. That's what mattered.

And it was nice. It was all so *nice*. The kind of joy that used to come so naturally around these people.

And then, like a needle scratching across the record of our evening, a familiar frame appeared in the doorway.

"Guess who's back?" Adam said, stepping in with duffel bags and a grin that felt too wide. Too confident. Like he'd walked in on cue. He flashed a grin, "Permanently."

Liv beamed with excitement, practically bouncing. "Really? You mean it?"

Adam shot her a wink. "Course, little Livvy."

Liv practically flung herself at him, not wasting a moment.

Josie nodded absently, completely uninterested. "Hi, Adam."

I did the mental math: twenty eight. He'd left for college at twenty-four, which... yeah, that tracked. But logic didn't make it feel any less strange. Any less *loaded*.

And it definitely didn't make it feel *safe*.

I didn't say anything. Neither did Izzie.

There was something in the way Adam said it. Like it was a claim. Or a warning.

He threw himself onto Liv's bed with that same smug ease, like he'd never left. Like he hadn't made a dent in everyone's timelines just by existing.

My body moved before I could think. I slipped off the bed and onto the floor beside Izzie, needing distance, needing *something*.

Liv didn't even seem to notice. She was still smiling, still glowing like the universe had just handed her something precious.

"No more running," Adam promised. "No more disappearing."

Izzie glanced up, meeting his gaze like it cost her something. She looked back down the moment his eyes locked on hers, and she picked at an old scab for a few beats. "Not going anywhere, then?"

Adam smirked, offering her a nod. "You're much older now. And no, sweet girl, I'm here to stay."

Izzie's jaw clenched – just slightly. Just enough for me to catch it.

And Liv, bless her, looked between us and asked the most oblivious thing in the world: "Isn't this the best news ever?"

I met her smile. Matched it. But it felt paper-thin. "Yeah," I said.

Sure. Best news ever.

Adam rose from the bed, stretching his arms out. "Well, I'm gonna go unpack my bags and see Mum, little Livvy," he announced, smiling at all of us. "Bye."

"Bye," Josie and I said in unison.

Izzie stood up then, sliding her phone into the pocket of her hoodie. "I've gotta go home."

I frowned. "Why?"

"I told Liv I have plans with Billy tonight." She offered me a half-smile, heading straight for the door. "I'll see you guys at school on Monday."

"Okay." I nodded. "Bye, Izzie."

"Bye, Savannah."

Then she disappeared into Liv's hallway.

"She's meeting up with Billy?" Josie asked, tilting her head to look at Liv. "Are they back on?"

Liv shrugged. "Never have a clue. I think he's with that girl he hooked up with." She tapped her chin, thinking. "What's her name? Oh, Daisy."

"Really?" Josie raised an eyebrow. "Because I catch Billy and Izzie together very often."

Liv's green eyes widened. "That… doesn't sound good." Then, brightening the mood, she added, "Can you guys stay over tonight? We have to celebrate somehow."

Josie nodded. "Sure."

I smiled too, my silent way of agreeing.

We settled in easily. Liv immediately flicked the TV on, some tragic romance that always had the power to make her cry beginning.

Josie was already asleep beside me, and Liv's head was resting gently on my shoulder, blonde curls flying everywhere.

Every so often, she'd laugh at something on the screen. And for a little while, it felt like before.

Before *everything*.

I glanced over to Liv's wardrobe, in desperate need of another blanket after Josie stole the other three. My eyes landed on something, something achingly familiar.

Marlee's letter.

Well, Liv's letter.

The air in the room changed. Or maybe I did. Because suddenly, everything felt tighter. Like the quiet was holding its breath.

It reminded me of just how long I'd left it sitting for. It reminded me that I couldn't do that for much longer.

But it felt scary.

Still, I needed to face it.

I needed to face it soon.

THE DREADED WORDS

AUGUST 14TH 2004

SAVANNAH

The familiar letter stared back at me as if it were pleading.

Not just *read me,* but *hear me. Finish me. Face me.*

Because this was Marlee.

And she deserved to be heard.

If it had been any of us in her place, she would've read it. She would've sat with the pain, even if it nearly swallowed her whole. She would've stayed up for days, tracing the ink with her fingers if it meant getting one inch closer to the truth.

She would've never walked away from me. Not in the way I had from her.

It had almost been a year and a half.

That was already far too long.

And if I didn't read it, I'd be taking that chance away from Marlee. Away from the girl who would never have hesitated to do the same for me.

So, I picked it up with shaky hands, hoping that maybe, this time I'd be strong enough to read it. To hear what pushed her over the edge.

God, it was hard.

But this wasn't about me.

This was about Marlee.

I slid the letter into my hand, opening it before I had the chance to put it somewhere far, far away.

I reread every line of what I'd seen, and swallowed hard before continuing from there.

It was Adam Coleman. I can't tell you a lot of the story, because that story is not mine to tell. But what I can tell you is that he hurt me.

My breath stopped.

No, no, no.

I had hoped, stupidly, that maybe I'd imagined that part. That maybe the feeling I got in my stomach was just my own imagination.

But no. It was real. She was talking about *him.*

For me, it was only a month ago. But there is so much to the story, Savannah, and I am sorry I can't tell you everything.

My fingers clenched around the letter. A tear slipped down my cheek before I even realised I was crying.

She blamed herself.

She blamed herself.

God.

The words blurred for a second, so I blinked hard, forcing myself to keep reading. To honour her voice, even when it split mine apart.

I want to see that it wasn't my fault, but I can't do that. It doesn't seem possible.

I never told you because I didn't know how. I was scared. I didn't want to lose everything, and I didn't want to see the day where nobody believed the truth. My truth. Telling people made it feel real, and I didn't want that. But it was real.

Whatever you do, don't blame Liv. She didn't know. I made the decision a while ago not to tell her. I didn't want to ruin her life, and I knew she couldn't handle it. Maybe, when you read this, she will be able to handle it.

You can tell her if you believe she should know. That's not my call anymore.

I didn't know.

I didn't know anything.

On another note, you should know that I believe you now. About your dad. I should have believed you the second you told me. I didn't. I questioned you and made you feel alone. I'll regret that forever. You were brave and I let you down. I'm sorry.

I was too blinded by my own struggles to realise how much you were going through. All I can hope is that when you finally read this, you're safe. I hope you managed to find happiness.

Savannah, I am sorry. I wish I could be stronger and stay for you, but I'm not. I've tried everything I could think of, but nothing helps.

This is my only option.

I know I'm young. I heard many of the speeches on how I still have so much ahead of me. I don't believe that's true.

I believe you will go places, Savannah. You will go far. All of you will. If Izzie ever manages to find peace in herself, I believe she will also change the world.

Again, I need you to know that this isn't your fault. You were one of my favourite people in the world. No, you were my world. I am so incredibly sorry to leave you with so many unanswered questions, but the one thing you can hold onto is the fact that I loved you.

When you remember me, don't think of the end. Please, remember the times we laughed together, and the times I stuck by your side. Remember me as the friend you loved, not the one who left. That's the person I always tried to be for you. Somebody worth loving.

I love you, Savannah. You saved my life a million times, and I thank you so deeply.

I am so sorry.

-   *Marlee xx*

My hands were still shaking when I read the last line. My eyes burned, but I couldn't cry. It was like my brain couldn't process what I just read.

She was right. I didn't need any more information to know what he did to her. It was clear, *very* clear, and I felt sick to my stomach.

I couldn't stop rereading the lines, hoping I'd misread something, but the words never changed. Every word spelled it out.

I hadn't seen any of it. She carried this alone for the entire month before her death, and I missed every sign.

I should have seen the signs.

I pressed the letter to my chest, finally letting the tears fall freely.

Fuck.

I missed it all.

And Adam... I knew there was something off about him. Deep down, I knew that.

But he wasn't just creepy or cruel. He was a monster. The villain in Marlee's story. A villain in a small town that still saw him as golden.

And now? He was home. In Ridgewood. For good.

And I couldn't change that.

Was I meant to tell Liv?

Was I not?

Was I meant to go to the police?
Was I not?
Oh God, what was I supposed to do?
I wanted to hit something.
I wanted to go back and do everything differently.
But all I could do was sit.
And cry.
And whisper her name.
"Marlee…"
I'm so sorry.
I'll do something.
I swear I will.

WE'LL FIGURE IT OUT

AUGUST 14TH 2004

ARCHIE

It was 11pm when the doorbell rang.

I wasn't sure who would be showing up this late, but I hopped out of bed immediately. Nobody showed up this late unless it was important. Urgent. Maybe even catastrophic.

I assumed it would've been one of Mum's clients—wouldn't be the first time they'd shown up in the middle of the night.

I always found it strange, considering Mum was always dead asleep by nine, but apparently, her clients didn't know how to show up during normal hours. Or maybe they didn't care. Desperation does that to people.

But it felt different.

Her clients usually pounded on the door like the world was ending. They were desperate, shaking, panicked.

But now?

There was only one knock.

One soft knock.

Barely audible, like whoever was out there wasn't sure if they deserved to be answered.

I padded softly to the front door, my feet cold against the wooden floor. I peeked through the peephole, and the second I saw her, I felt my heart drop.

Sav.

Why was she at my house during the night?

Why now?

Shit. This couldn't be good.

I flung the door open the moment I saw her face. Her grey eyes were red and puffy, her cheeks tear-stained and hollowed with grief.

"Sav?" I whispered, trying to keep my voice calm and hide the panic rushing through me. "What's wrong?"

She didn't answer. Instead, she dropped her head to her hands, her body trembling as fresh tears streamed down her face.

I didn't need to know what happened. I just needed to keep her safe.

I *always* needed to keep her safe.

"Sav," I said her name soothingly, gently running my hand through her hair, the other one resting around her waist. "Did something happen?"

She nodded once.

"Do you wanna talk about it?"

Another nod.

Without another word, I kept my arm around her waist and guided her up the stairs, tiptoeing past Mum's room. I didn't know exactly what was going on yet, but I knew it was the kind of thing she didn't need an audience for.

She immediately sat on my bed, and I joined her quietly. I didn't know if she needed words, if she needed a hug, or if she just needed silence.

"I'm scared," Sav admitted quietly, sniffling against my shoulder. "And I n-need to tell you."

"Okay." I nodded, her words worrying me further. "You can tell me."

"I can't." She shook her head, reaching into the pocket of her jeans. She pulled out an envelope, one with a very familiar name. A name I hadn't expected to see tonight. "Read it. Please, because I can't—I can't say it."

"Alright," I responded, trying impossibly hard to keep my voice soft so she didn't break further. But... fuck. I had Marlee's letter in my hand. "Are you sure you want me to read this, Sav?"

"Please, Archie," she begged, voice more audible now. "I need you to read it."

I blew out a shaky breath, sliding the letter out of the envelope.

It was heavier than paper had ever felt, but I knew why. These words were going to be the heaviest I'd ever read.

At first, I wasn't sure what to focus on. Marlee's handwriting, her face in my mind, or Sav's sobs from beside me.

I almost couldn't bear to read it. But I needed to be strong. Somebody else needed to be strong this time. Sav had done enough of that for three lifetimes.

It took everything in me to keep reading, but I did. Word by word, line by line, until I'd read it all.

Then I just sat there.

I couldn't look at Sav yet. I knew if I did, I'd lose it.

Instead, I looked down at the floor, the letter trembling in my hands. "Jesus Christ," I whispered, unsure of what to do. Unsure of *everything*.

Adam. Fucking Adam.

I felt fucking sick. I wanted to say I couldn't believe it, but that was the problem. I wholeheartedly believed it, and that only made the whole situation worse. The way somebody we knew could be so evil was beyond me.

The guy had always been word, and I never liked him. I wouldn't feel great about him being around Sav, but fuck. I didn't expect this.

And Marlee never told anybody. Not until it was too late, anyway.

Fuck.

"I didn't know," she whispered, like she needed to say it out loud to believe it. Like she needed me to believe it.

"I know," I replied quietly, because what was I supposed to say? Of course she didn't know. There was no fucking way she could know something like that about her friend and keep it to herself. But I had no bloody words.

With no fucking idea of what to do next, I squeezed a little tighter on her hand. She leaned into my touch, not uttering another word. I wasn't sure either of us could.

"Izzie read Marlee's letter," she murmured against my shoulder, wiping her tears. "She must know."

I nodded in agreement.

Her sobs loudened, and she rested her entire body weight on my shoulder like she could barely hold herself up any more.

I was very close to feeling the same.

I don't know how long we sat there for. All I know is that everything was different now. There was before we read that letter, and now, there was after.

And nothing about this part felt okay.

"Stay over." I heard myself say, desperate to keep her around.

"Yeah," she replied emptily, offering me a tiny, barely visible nod. "Don't make me go home, Archie. I need- I just…" She dropped her head to her hands again. "Oh god."

"I know," I soothed. "I know."

We sat there for at least half an hour before moving to the top of my bed, both of us resting our heads on the same pillow.

"What am I supposed to do, Archie? Sav asked, eyes still puffy, but free of tears. "There's so much… so much I should do."

"No." I shook my head, pulling her in closer. "Don't let yourself carry this burden alone."

She nodded slowly. "Okay."

"Hey." I tilted her chin upward, making her look into my eyes. "You couldn't have stopped this from happening to her, and you can't change it now."

"I know." She offered me a weak smile. "It's scary, though. Liv loves him."

My eyes widened slightly, and I swallowed. "Do you think…"

"No," she said honestly, clearly understanding what I meant. "I really, really don't."

"Good," I responded, letting out a heavier breath. "At least that."

"At least that," she repeated in a whisper. "Archie?"

"Yeah?"

"You were the first person I came to," she told me, biting down on her lip as she always did when things became too much. "You were the only person I needed to see."

"What does that mean?" I tilted her head.

"It means I let you in," she explained, letting out a short laugh. "I did, Archie. You're the only one I never wanted to run away from."

"Yeah?" I asked, smiling slightly, even though the ache of Marlee's letter was lingering in my mind. "Thanks."

"Thanks you," she whispered tiredly, laughing at her own words. "I just made… um, I made an out loud spelling mistake."

I chuckled despite myself. "Yeah, baby. You did."

Her head tilted up to look at me again, realising the weight of my words at the same time I did.

I immediately shook my head. "Sorry."

"Don't be sorry," she replied, resting her head on my chest now. "Thank you."

I laughed against her hair, pressing a soft kiss to it. "That's perfectly fine."

I allowed my eyes to close before forcing them open once more. "Hey, Sav? Once we figure all of this out, we should go on a real date."

Nothing.

I moved my head, wondering what she was thinking.

Sav was asleep.

I chuckled, pressing a soft, lingering kiss to her forehead. "We'll figure it out."

BEGIN AGAIN

AUGUST 17TH 2004

SAVANNAH

I only read Marlee's letter a few days ago, but it felt like forever ago. Every minute since that day, I'd been thinking about her words. About the fact I hadn't noticed.

But after a million conversations with Archie over the past few days, I'd come to the realisation that I couldn't have stopped this from happening.

That didn't stop the ache, but it helped clear my mind just enough to figure out what the next step was.

Apparently, I decided the step *before* that was to go on a date with Archie. He asked me when we woke up at his house the next morning—his voice still raspy from sleep, his arms still around me like I was something to protect – and I hadn't even thought about it before saying yes.

There were no questions when it came to him, I realised.

I just wanted him. All of him.

Plus, he was the only one with the ability to slow my mind down, even if only for a moment, and allow me to think straight.

We were at the same restaurant we came to on our date-not-date last time. It was just as gorgeous as I remembered. The dim lighting in our private room managed to calm the beat of my heart just slightly. The candle between us flickered gently, casting golden shadows across his features. I could still hear faint music playing through the restaurant speakers, but it was soft enough that I didn't need to focus on it.

It was nice.

Peaceful, even, in that delicate sort of way – like glass on the verge of shattering.

"You good?" Archie asked, pulling me away from my thoughts.

"Yeah," I whispered, and it wasn't even a lie. Sure, I was heartbroken about Marlee's letter, but there were positives too, right? I had Archie across from me, after all.

But that didn't stop it.

I had Archie. Even if we weren't anything official, I knew I had him. And he'd had me for a while. Still, the ache of the truth hit me like a bus each time I allowed myself to feel happiness.

"I'm not sure," I corrected myself with a small shrug. "But we're here, and I'm trying. That has to count for something."

He smiled proudly. "That absolutely counts for something."

I smiled as he reached his hand across the table, nervously tucking a loose wave behind my ear. "I like when your waves are out."

"Yeah?" I tilted my head, more grateful than I cared to show.

It was rare for me to let my natural hair out when we lived at home. I sometimes did, but more often than not, I'd straighten it. Or tie it up until you couldn't tell.

I was never sure why. Now that I realised my waves didn't come from my father, but from my real parents, it felt less eerie to show them.

I glanced around the restaurant, at all of these people who looked like they had their lives together, and realised I was truly free now.

Maybe I'd never feel complete, maybe I'd struggle for the rest of my life, but I was a survivor. I could see that now.

Marlee was a survivor too, until the day she decided surviving wasn't enough.

I didn't blame her. I really didn't.

It wouldn't be fair of me to blame my friend for giving up on life when I knew exactly how it felt to feel that was the only way out.

I just wished she'd given life a longer chance, because Marlee was Marlee. She always told us about the amazing things we'd do someday, but I truly believed she would.

Marlee, more than anyone, was genuine. She was beautiful, intelligent, and kind hearted. Marlee McGovern wouldn't have hurt a fly. That only made the fact that Adam hurt her more screwed up.

Because Marlee wouldn't have fought back. I knew she wouldn't have, because she was a slightly more outgoing version of me.

I never would have fought back either, but she never should have been in a position where she needed to fight back.

It wasn't fair.

"What am I supposed to do?" I suddenly asked, needing the answers to questions I wasn't even sure of. "I mean… I just don't know what comes next."

He nodded in understanding, swallowing his bite of steak before meeting my eyes. "There's nothing set in stone, Sav. There's nothing certain here. But you do have choices."

"What choices?" I shrugged helplessly, hoping he had better answers than I did.

"You can tell somebody," Archie offered, the worried look in his eyes telling me that he knew how hard that could be. "You were close with her Mum, yeah? You could talk to her. You could tell Liv…" He trailed off, thinking to himself for a beat. "You could talk to Izzie."

"Izzie?" I tilted my head.

"You said it yourself, Izzie's the only other person who read the letter," he explained. "Maybe she can help."

"If Izzie knows and kept it to herself this whole time, that means she doesn't wanna take action for whatever reason," I told him, sighing. "Her opinion won't change just because I know the truth now."

"That's true," he agreed. "So, what about speaking to her Mum?"

"Lila?" I asked, more to myself than him. "Isn't that a really big step?"

"Yeah, look, I wish I could tell you this will be easy." His green eyes locked on mine, full of something heavier than sadness. "It will be really bloody hard, Sav. You... you just need to think about it before you make any big decisions. You're in control here."

"Being in control is scary."

"Yeah," he agreed with a frown. "It's very scary, but you're not running out of time. You can think about it, then decide."

I nodded, then slapped a hand over my face. "I'm sorry. This is supposed to be a date, but I'm rambling on."

"Please," he scoffed. "As if I'd ask you to stop speaking about Marlee. You never have to choose your words carefully, Sav. Not with me. You're being honest, and that makes me prouder than I can even put into words."

I smiled at his words. "Thank you."

"You're special, Sav. You're not like everybody else," he told me, voice warm. "Marlee was right. You're gonna go far."

My smile softened as I sipped on my diet coke. "Don't flatter me."

"I will flatter you every day for the rest of our lives, and I'll mean it." He shot me a wink before realising the weight of his words, and letting out a surprised chuckle. "Bit far for the first date, huh?"

"*Technical* first date," I corrected him with a grin. "Also, if I'm not awkward around you, we're definitely past the 'taking back our words' face. Because I'm awkward around everyone."

"You were never awkward around me."

"I was absolutely awkward around you," I giggled, getting embarrassed at the memories. "I quite literally jumped into your car when I barely knew you."

"Knew what ya wanted, huh," he snickered.

"I didn't." I shook my head, smiling softly at him. "I know now."

"I'm gonna vomit right over the two of ya," a familiar voice announced, and there was only one person who sounded that dramatically disgusted.

"Theo." I grinned immediately.

His entire face softened. "Savvy. How are you doing?"

"I'm…" I trailed off, still not having a perfect answer. But when my eyes met Archie's again, I knew the truth. "I'm good, Theo."

"Good." He smiled. "Freedom looks wonderful on you."

"Are ya hitting on my…" Archie trailed off, frowning to himself. "Are ya hitting on Sav?"

Theo let out a wheezy laugh. "Absolutely, bud. I'm always hitting on her."

Archie rolled his eyes, standing from his seat. "I gotta use the bathroom," he announced, eyes flicking to Theo. "Keep her company, will ya?"

"With pleasure," Theo snickered, causing Archie to flip him off before heading to the bathroom by the back of the restaurant.

"How are you and Liv going?" I asked casually.

He scoffed. "We're… going."

My eyes widened, head snapping up immediately. "You are?"

"No," he mumbled. "We're not."

"I don't get it." I shook my head, utterly confused. "The two of you are blatantly obvious. What's holding you back?"

"Nothing," he said. "There's nothing holding me back. Hey, don't accuse me. Maybe she's the reason we're not together."

I giggled. "Okay."

He frowned for a moment, then joined in on the laughter. "You're my very favourite friend after Bennett, you know that?"

I grinned. "You're my very favourite too."

"Didn't steal her?" Archie called out, finally arriving back at our table.

"Like you'd let that happen, Cap," Theo teased, but there was honesty behind it. "As long as I can keep the racoon."

Archie's head snapped up. "What raccoon?"

"The one we agreed to parent." Theo's brows furrowed together, looking frustrated as Archie clearly had no idea what he was talking about. "Julia. The fucking racoon, Cap."

Archie ran a hand down in his face, taking a seat across from me. "That was not me that ya called, bud."

"Who did I call, then?"

"Danny." He blew out a long breath. "You asked if he and…"

"Fucking hell. I asked if he and Izzie wanted to parent her, didn't I?"

"Yeah."

"And you didn't stop me?"

"I wasn't with ya!"

"And that's where the problem begins."

Theo rolled his eyes.

"Alright, fuck off, will ya?" Archie said, but his tone was laced with that fondness only a best friend can get away with.

Theo scurried off, throwing one final wink at me before disappearing around the corner.

Archie turned back to me. "Let's get you home, huh?" he asked, nodding toward my arm. I looked down to see goosebumps, unnoticed until now.

"Okay," I agreed, smiling genuinely. "Thanks."

He hooked his arm through mine, and my smile only grew. "Huh. Chivalry isn't dead," I snickered, tilting my head up to look at him.

I found him already staring, something soft and unreadable in his eyes.

Then he kissed me.

It was short, but everything.

His lips pressed gently to mine – tender, yet certain – and I felt my chest expand with something I hadn't let myself feel in a long time.

Hope.

When he pulled back, I took a shaky breath.

"Yeah," he whispered, more to himself than me. "We'll figure it out."

HURT PEOPLE HURT PEOPLE

AUGUST 21ST 2004

SAVANNAH

I knew Theo and Izzie didn't get along. I did.

But it wasn't always like that. Theo and Izzie used to be good friends.

It was a common misconception that he had simply been included on her list of many enemies after Marlee's death. That was entirely wrong.

It had started a long while before that, and it never seemed to stop.

Still, I hadn't expected it to happen in the middle of the gym.

I wasn't there. Not really.

I showed up near the end of what looked like a war, and came face to face with an half-angry, half-distraught Izzie, and Theo looking more resigned than I'd ever seen him.

The others arrived at the same time as me—but none of us had heard the whole thing.

Still, I managed to end up in the principal's office. Other than Billy, the others had been left out of this. I assumed they asked us to attend for moral support.

"You need to drop this, Isobel Harris," Mrs. Brown warned, shaking her head firmly. "It is absolutely unacceptable."

"I didn't lay a hand on him," came Izzie's defensive response.

"I never said that you did," Mrs. Brown replied. "Isobel, physical assault is not the only thing we strive to erase. You have been harassing Mr. Callahan since the beginning of time, and you must know that we won't accept it for much longer."

Izzie let out a humourless laugh, but that couldn't erase the tears welling up in her eyes. Her body was coiled like a spring, her jaw clenched tight enough to break teeth."What, are you gonna expel me for making a few *comments*?"

"You accused him of rape, Isobel."

Izzie scoffed, glaring at Theo. "I absolutely did nothing of the sort. I accused him of being a *witness*."

There it was. Her voice cracked – not with guilt, but with something darker. Fury. Betrayal. Her hands trembled, and I could see it – the way her knuckles turned white.

Fuck.

"I was not a witness," Theo muttered absently, dropping his head to his hands.

"Theodore, where is this coming from?" Mrs. Brown questioned, looking genuinely confused.

So was I.

171

But this, without a doubt, had something to do with Marlee. I just couldn't figure out what.

"Grey." Her eyes flickered to me. "Do you have any idea of this situation? I'm not sure why they insisted we have you in here."

"To stop any fights." I shrugged, throwing her my best guess. "I don't have anything to say. I'll just... sit here."

She raised an eyebrow, but after taking another glance at the two of them, she gladly nodded. "Thank you."

I offered her a small, short smile before glancing back at my angry friend. "Izzie—" I tried, but she was quick to interrupt.

"No," she cut in, voice rough. "Let me speak, Savannah. This is just one thing on a long list of many things he's fucked up."

"You're fucking crazy," Theo added, head still in his hands.

"I am not crazy!" Izzie snapped, running a helpless hand down her face. "I'm not fucking crazy. I'm tired of that word. I was labeled that because nobody understood. Everybody's blind!"

"Iz—" That was Billy.

Usually he could calm her down, but she was different today. Something else had snapped inside of her.

"No!" Her voice raised, almost as if she was begging for somebody to hear her. "Why won't anybody listen to me!"

"It's over, Izzie!" Theo shouted, looking utterly devastated as well as put-up. "It. Is. Over."

"It's never over!" Izzie responded, voice raising to a volume that caused everybody in the room to flinch. She threw her hands over her head, letting her body collapse into Billy's arms. "Fuck," she sobbed.

There was nothing left of the composed girl I knew. She looked shattered—wild-eyed and broken, like something had clawed her apart from the inside.

"Theo," Billy attempted to reason with him, but I could tell he was done.

While I loved Izzie, I certainly couldn't blame Theo for this.

"I don't have any pity left for her," he replied, shrugging. "I really fucking don't."

"Maybe you just need to—" Mrs. Brown tried.

"All of you shut up!" Theo cut in, taking a careful step away from the room. His blue eyes flickered to Izzie, still sobbing in Billy's arms. "You are fucking insane."

"Theo!"

"Don't ya worry." He shook his head. "I'm going."

Once Theo left the room, I darted around, hoping somebody could give me any sort of an explanation. I glanced at Billy, my eyes asking him every question I couldn't voice.

He didn't say anything. Just shook his head like he felt as helpless as I did.

I stood there for a moment longer, lingering by the glass doors that Theo had just stormed out of. I wasn't sure if I was supposed to stay or leave, so I made no sudden moves.

"You can go," Billy clarified, letting out a heavy sigh as he saw the broken look in Izzie's eyes. "I've got her."

I hesitated for a moment, but smiled slightly when I realised who I was talking to. "I know you do," I whispered, and walked away as quickly as humanly possible.

I needed to get far, far away.

There weren't many days where I struggled to understand Izzie Harris. But today was one of them.

The worst part? I'd only seen the aftermath. I couldn't begin to imagine what led them there. I wasn't sure if I wanted to.

And now, I needed to figure out what the hell I was supposed to do.

"It's so much worse now," I declared, heading straight into my brother's room once I arrived home. "I don't understand the hatred Izzie has for him, Jay."

"The curly-head bloke?" Jayden asked, not missing a beat. "She's still on that?"

I tilted my head to the side. "How do you know about that?"

"Come on, Sav," he chuckled just slightly. "That war has been going on for years now."

"Yeah," I agreed, glad to speak to somebody who had also witnessed it. I flopped down on his bed, blowing out a long breath. "I just don't understand. I swear, she was ready to kill him today."

"Izzie's head doesn't work the same way ours do," my brother explained, but I already knew that. Still, I allowed him to continue. "She's royally fucked up, and it's probably not her fault."

I nodded in agreement. "I know."

"Hurt people hurt people, Sav." Jayden shrugged helplessly, running a hand down his face like he was searching for answers. "Maybe that doesn't justify it, but do ya remember how much of a dick I was?"

"What, last year?" I laughed through the soft cries. "Yeah, I remember."

There was a long pause. Not the awkward kind – the heavy kind, filled with all the things we never said aloud.

"Point in question," he agreed with a nod. "Izzie's not a bad person underneath it all, and you know that better than anyone. That makes sense to me. I just don't know what he could have done to make her so fucking angry towards him."

"It's Theo," I stated like that explained everything. To me, it did. "Theo's wonderful. I truly doubt that he purposely hurt her."

"Maybe it wasn't on purpose," Jayden whispered, laying down beside me. "Maybe he just… said something."

I chuckled, wiping away the tears before looking at him in disbelief. "You think he said something, and that's why she wants to murder him?"

"Yeah, not my best idea," Jayden agreed. "I've got no fucking clue, Savvy."

"She said he was a witness of rape," I confided. "I really don't believe that. But I think…" I turned my head just enough to see his entire face. "I really think she believes it, Jay."

He raised an eyebrow. "What rape?"

My lips parted, but quickly closed again.

Shit.

I hadn't told him about Marlee.

Suddenly, there were tears streaming down my face, and my entire body went limp. "This wasn't supposed to happen, Jay," I sobbed, my body weight relying on my big brother to keep me up. "I was supposed to read her note and feel better. She wasn't… I just didn't…"

"Shh," Jayden soothed, still confused as he held me close. "Savvy, slow down, okay?"

"Marlee," I choked out, crying like a small child. "Her letter."

His eyes immediately darkened. "What did it tell you, Savvy?"

"Adam." I hiccuped a sob, willing myself to continue before I lost the courage. "He… um…"

"He raped her." He squeezed his eyes shut, catching onto my words before I even finished the sentence. "He fucking raped her."

"Yeah," I confirmed between sobs.

Jayden went still. Completely still.

The kind of still that only comes from people who've lived through hell. I saw it flicker behind his eyes – the old ghosts, our parents, the screaming, the blood, the silence.

I'd never seen him like this. Not even after Mum and Dad died. Not even when he was destroyed after finding out Mum was pregnant with Aidan.

"I'll kill him," he told me, voice rough and venomous.

"Jay—" I tried, but he was already pacing the room like a madman.

"No, Savvy. I mean it. I'll fucking kill him," he added. "He doesn't get to rape a girl and drive her to suicide, and continue walking around like nothing ever fucking happened!"

I wiped my face with my sleeve. "You can't do anything, Jay. Don't sink to his level."

"Sink to his level, Savvy?" Jayden shook his head. "What, do you expect me to sit here and do nothing?"

"I'll come up with a plan," I told him. "I will. Just… Please give me time."

"Fuck," he muttered, then again, louder, "*Fuck.*"

I nodded, swallowing the lump in my throat. "I know. I'll… I will figure something out."

I *had* to.

And I meant it. Because this didn't end with Marlee. This was bigger. This was the start of something terrible – and it was only just beginning.

GRAVES DON'T LIE
AUGUST 28TH 2004

ARCHIE

Sav had practically been MIA for the whole week.

She'd sent a few messages here and there – just enough to prove she was alive – but they weren't the kind of messages that made me feel better. I'd stopped trying to push her after day three. At that point, all I could do was wait.

And maybe, if this were any other time, I would've chalked it up to normal teenage burnout. God knows we were all due for a few off days. But this wasn't that.

It had to have something to do with Marlee. That guilt? The kind that chews you up from the inside? I knew it too well.

Because while our circumstances were very, *very* different, I'd been the same after Elsie and Dad died.

The weight of it. The wondering. That stupid voice in your head that won't stop asking *"What if you'd done something different?"*

I was in the car that night. I thought I should've stopped it. I should've *known*.

But knowing doesn't fix anything.

I didn't eat. I didn't sleep. I could barely look anyone in the eye.

And it took *years* – actual years – for me to finally say the words: "It wasn't my fault."

Now? I needed Sav to get to that point. Even if it took everything in me.

So, I did the only thing I could.

I showed up at her house.

Adele and Jason had invited me in about fifteen minutes ago, and they'd been talking my ear off about "dating rules" ever since. The irony was not lost on me. I wasn't even dating their daughter.

Not technically.

Still, I smiled. Nodded. Pretended I was paying more attention than I was.

Because all I could think was: *Please be okay, Sav. Please don't be falling apart without anyone there to catch you.*

"I'm gonna go check on Sav if that's okay," I said finally, standing.

Jason gave a tight nod, but it was Adele who smiled and said, "She's been on the warpath. I think having you here will be wonderful for her."

Hearing that only alarmed me more, so I rushed for the stairs.

Jayden was there. Towering at the top like a damn sentry.

The infamous big brother. Terrifying. Loyal. Protective. A human baseball bat wrapped in tattoos and trauma.

"Jayden," I said, nodding. I tried not to sound nervous.

Sure, I'd met him before.

But now? I was showing up at his house because I knew I was the only one who could calm his baby sister down.

He narrowed his eyes. "Bennett. Here for my sister, I assume?"

"I am."

"And can I trust you with her?" Came his cynical response. Yet, I couldn't judge him. They'd grown up in a certain way that causes you to be distrustful.

I didn't flinch. "She trusts me."

His eyes locked on mine for a second longer than I was comfortable with, and then – to my absolute shock – he *grinned*.

"Good response, bud."

I blinked. "Yeah?"

"Yeah. Also, please tell your creepy blonde friend to stop texting me about making him fucking cupcakes."

I barked a laugh, relief washing over me like a tide. "Theo?"

He gave a noncommittal shrug. "The freak with the smile. Probably."

I gave him a thumbs up. "Will do."

And then I bolted upstairs, the smile fading quickly.

Because I needed to see her.

I knocked once, but I wasn't greeted with Sav. No, just the girl that looked eerily similar to her. Brooke.

"Hi," I said, eyes darting around the room behind her. There was no sign of Sav. "Where is she?" I asked, voice quieter, just in case.

Brooke pointed to the bathroom before saying, "You can try, but she's been in there all day. I'll go downstairs and give you some space."

"Thank you," I whispered, watching her disappear like a ghost.

I made my way through their impressively large room and stopped once I reached the ensuite in the corner. "Sav?" I whispered, pressing my ear to the door.

One sob. "Archie?" she whispered shakily.

"Yeah," I squeezed my eyes closed. "It's me."

The door opened so fast I barely had time to register her before her arms wrapped tight around me. Desperate. Like she thought I might vanish too.

I held her back just as hard.

"Are you okay?" I asked, pulling back just enough to see her face. Her eyes were puffy. Her hair was knotted at the ends. But she was here. That was enough. "Talk to me, Sav. I'm here."

She sank onto the edge of the bed closest to the window. "I'm probably worrying them. I didn't mean to. I just... I needed everything to stop for a second."

I shook my head, squeezing her hand in reassurance. "Stop worrying about everybody else, Sav. Worry about yourself."

She frowned. "I think I might have forgotten how to do that."

"I've got you," I promised, squeezing her hand gently. "We'll figure it out."

"I'm just…" She bit the inside of her cheek, thinking to herself before she looked up at me with those wide, puppy-dog-eyes that told me she needed me to be strong this time. "I'm just a bit scared. I'm not quite sure what I'm supposed to do."

"I know," I replied, because I did know. There was nothing about this situation that made sense, and after the million questions I'd asked my Mum, expecting her to know the answers, I realised this was possibly the hardest situation to be in. "It fucking sucks that it's all on you."

"I don't think I want to do what Izzie did," she admitted in a whisper, shaking her head once. "I can't keep this to myself, Archie. I just can't."

"I think I want to tell someone."

"Okay."

She looked up. "Just like that?"

"Just like that." I kissed her temple. "Whatever you choose, I'm behind you. Always."

She exhaled shakily. "Hypothetically… if I told someone, like a real someone, would it go to court?"

"There's really no way of knowing," I immediately answered. "Realistically, they might see the situation as useless considering Marlee's death and the fact that there isn't enough proof. It's harsh, but some of the lawyers around here suck." Seeing the defeated look on her small face, I added, "But, that's not a definite. You have a handwritten letter from Marlee, and you also have a million people in your corner."

She nodded, silently pleading with her eyes for me to continue.

So, I did. "For whatever reason, it all works differently around here. Even though none of you actually witnessed the event, or that we know of, they would still have you all testify against him."

She tilted her head, sniffling quietly. "What would that do?"

"They'd get you to testify, as well as everybody else who received a letter." I continued. "That would give us a much better chance of getting that dick locked up forever but…"

"Izzie and Liv would have to agree." Her grey eyes widened, clearly realising the weight of this situation. "Shit."

"Yeah," I whispered in agreement. "Shit."

"I'm not saying I wanna do anything yet," she clarified, looking at me with desperate eyes. "But if I was to get Izzie on board, and Liv believes me, this could go through as a real case?"

I just looked at her, hoping she would catch on before I needed to explain further.

"Lila McGovern," she added, not missing a beat. "Shit, I didn't even think about her Mum. We'd have to get her on board, right?"

I nodded, confirming her words. "She might not know, Sav. But Marlee and her got along well, right?"

"Right."

"Then I'm sure she'd love to see that fucker behind bars," I told her with a smile I could only hoped brought her a sense of comfort.

"Yeah," she whispered, smiling back. "Yeah, you're right."

Marlee wasn't gone. Just buried.

YOU'LL BE SEEING ME

SEPTEMBER 4TH 2004

ARCHIE

Tonight was supposed to be easy.

My seventeenth birthday. The plan was for me, Sav, and our strange group of friends to show up at my place and have a small party.

Keyword: small.

Apparently, nobody got that memo.

Right now, I had at least four hundred drunk people running around my house like it was a bloody basketball court.

I could only be thankful to my Mum for choosing to spend a few nights away over my Birthday, because I'd be bloody dead if she were here.

"Archie," Sav whispered, giggling slightly. "A small party?"

"Yeah." I dropped my head, attempting to block out the noise. Failed. "That was the plan."

She smiled, and that was all I needed to forget the fact that my entire house was being ripped to fucking shreds.

Lately, it had been hard to forget about Marlee. Ever since I found out the truth, I felt fucking sick.

The situation was utterly screwed up, and there was no denying that.

But tonight? Tonight was my night, but I wasn't the only one around here who needed to forget.

"Drink?" I winked, offering Sav a ridiculously bright red cup. "It'll help with the nerves."

"I know how alcohol works, Archie," she fired back, causing me to grin like a bloody idiot. Savannah Grey, against all my earlier thoughts, certainly had a sharp side to her, and I loved it. "And thanks," she added, taking the cup right from my hands.

I chuckled, offering her a nod. "Of course."

"Did Izzie end up coming?" She tilted her head, obviously worried about her angsty friend. "She's barely spoken to anyone this week."

"Izzie never speaks to anyone." I shrugged, subtly nodding toward the stairs. "She showed up."

Sav smiled at the sight of Izzie chatting with the only person we could have expected. Billy was smiling down at her, clearly fucking smitten despite the hell she put him through over the years.

"One strong bloke," I muttered beneath my breath, but Sav caught it.

"And you're not?" She raised an eyebrow, taking a short sip of her drink. "You stuck around."

"You're not insane."

"Some people would say the opposite," she said, laughing. "It doesn't really matter, though. Maybe Izzie and I have different stories, and different ways of coping, but that doesn't make hers any less important."

I sighed, smiling in agreement. She was always right. "Yeah, I know that."

"Some people struggle to tell the difference between a bad person, and a person who needs help," Sav continued, glancing in Izzie's direction. "She's not a bad person, Archie, but she is a hurt person. That doesn't mean she isn't good. Underneath it all, Izzie's a great girl."

I smiled. "I hope to see that side one day, then."

She matched my smile with one of her own. "You will."

Catching the conflicted look in her grey eyes, I frowned. "Something on your mind?"

"I don't want Izzie to hate me," she admitted quietly. "And I can't bear to see the look on Liv's face if I told her about Adam."

My eyes widened slightly, but I didn't let the surprise show. "Does that mean you're not going through with it?"

She quickly shook her head. "No. I still haven't decided. I'm just... scared."

"I think you're supposed to be scared," I offered. "And you're certainly allowed to be."

She nodded once. "Thanks, Archie."

"Seventeen, bud," Theo announced, bouncing up to me. "Happy birthday."

I chuckled. "Thanks."

"Hello," Theo greeted with a wink, attention flicking to Sav. "Ah, Savvy. Exactly the girl I was looking for."

"Why?" Sav replied, tilting her head in confusion. "Are you gonna do something weird?"

Theo huffed. "That's an awful assumption. And no, I was just gonna let you know I'll be staying at your house tomorrow."

Sav frowned, glaring at him. "At my house?"

"Yup," he confirmed casually, downing his beer in one sip.

"Don't you usually stay at Olivia's?" I cut in, thoroughly confused.

"Yeah," he agreed, sighing. "She's spending the night with her dick of a brother."

"And you can't join her?"

"No," he replied immediately, looking back down at Sav with puppy-dog eyes. "Please. I'll be good."

Sav rolled her eyes, but there was a fondness underneath it. "Okay, okay."

"No stealing my girlfriend." I heard myself mutter before realising what I'd just said. My eyes widened slightly as I looked down at Sav. "Not my girlfriend," I corrected nervously, glancing back at Theo. "No stealing Sav."

Theo chuckled at my mistake. "Alright bud."

"I'm gonna go find Liv," Sav announced with a laugh. Thankfully, she didn't seem weirded out by my comment.

She headed off immediately, and my best friend turned to me with a grin. "Your girlfriend?"

"No," I muttered. "My Sav, though."

"She's always been *your* Sav," Theo agreed, snatching my beer right from my hands. He took a swig, made a face, and handed it back. "Jesus, that's fucking disgusting. What is this? Battery acid?"

I didn't answer. I was too busy watching Sav disappear into the crowd, red cup still in hand, a slight bounce in her step as if she was trying to shake something off, or run toward something. Even now, it was hard to tell with her.

Theo huffed a laugh, patting me on the back. "You're thinking too much."

"Maybe I'm not thinking enough," I replied. "That's been half of my problem with her. That's how I missed everything with her parents."

His expression shifted to something more genuine once I said that. "You weren't supposed to know, Cap."

I let out a defeated sigh. "Yeah. I was."

He shook his head in protest. "No, because you never would have imagined something like that. If you haven't experienced abuse, it's hard to pick it in other people."

I nodded, thankful for his words. See? This was why he was my best friend. Not because he was a bloody idiot, or because he pissed me off 24/7, but because he was fiercely loyal when it counted.

I let my eyes scan the room, and instantly regretted that choice. Somebody had spilt something neon and fucking sticky all over the dining table, and Jayden, who had shown up an hour ago, was making a terrible effort at hiding the fact he was throwing up in Mum's favourite vase.

Delightful.

I groaned, pulling my eyes away from the sight.

"I might go find her," I murmured, scratching my jaw.

Theo didn't argue, he just nodded. "Go."

I pushed through a crowd of drunk girls with the entire bloody basketball team fawning over them, praying I didn't get knocked over, or, worse, vomited on.

Finally, I found her by the kitchen. The music was pounding, but it was by far the quietest place tonight.

"Hi." I smiled once I reached her, joining her behind the bench. "How ya doing?"

"Good," she replied, and this time, it didn't sound like a lie.

I allowed my eyes to scan her for a moment. She was wearing a little blue dress, and had eyeshadow the same colour. Fuck. Theo was right. Freedom did suit her.

"Wanna come upstairs?" I asked, desperate to escape the noise for a few minutes.

"Bit forward, are we?" she teased.

I laughed, my head leaning back slightly. "It's quieter up there."

"It's a party," she snickered, reaching for my hand. "Did you really expect quiet?"

"I guess not." I shrugged, not bothering to argue, because I could feel her hand in mine, and I needed her close more than I'd needed anything before. "What do you suggest then?"

She thought for a moment. "Dance with me."

"Yeah?" I raised an eyebrow, loving her suggestion. Or demand. Either way, I was in. "Let's do it."

As we headed to the makeshift dance floor in my living room, the speakers began blaring Maroon 5's *This Love.*

She laughed, throwing her head back as she did, and it was a bloody wonderful sight. One I needed to see more often.

As we pushed into the crowd of people that certainly were not dancers, it felt like the living room had doubled in size, or maybe it was just the amount of bodies packed into one space.

Either way, I barely noticed any of it.

Because Sav was in front of me, and she was dancing. Her hair was wild, waves poking out in every direction, but her eyes were locked on me as if I was the only other person in the room.

Sure, I'd seen her cheer, but fuck. I'd never seen her dance like this. Carefree. She looked more beautiful than ever.

And me? I was absolutely done for.

"This is chaos," I shouted over the music, voice hardly audible against it.

"You're the one who threw the party!" she yelled back, spinning to press her back against me.

The music crashed around us. Someone knocked into my back. A drink spilled nearby. But she didn't move, and neither did I.

"I suppose I'm glad this party didn't end up small," she announced, grinning up at me.

"As am I."

She laughed again, louder this time. "I should get going, Archie!"

I nodded in agreement, not liking the idea of her being around when the guys were too drunk to tell the difference between girls. "Okay."

"I'll be seeing you." She laughed, offering me a small wave.

"You'll be seeing me." I sighed in disbelief.

This was far from over.

LOVELY FAMILY, LONELY TRUTH

SEPTEMBER 5TH 2004

SAVANNAH

"You weren't joking about staying at my house," I laughed in disbelief, glancing down at Theo's blue sleeping bag.

"I was not," he confirmed with that grin he always wore.

I stepped to the side, allowing him in.

He came in immediately, spotting Jayden across the room. "I'm gonna go talk to my friend."

I raised an eyebrow. "Your friend?"

"Yup," he confirmed, making a beeline for my brother, who, to my surprise, didn't look half annoyed to see Theo.

I laughed at the sight, spotting Adele and Jason on the back patio. Whether I wanted to or not, I realised I needed to speak to them.

Right now, the boys were asleep, Brooke was next door, and Jayden was occupied by Theo.

This may have been my only chance, and I needed to take it.

"Hi," I whispered with a smile as I slid the back door open, joining Adele on the old couch. "Sorry I haven't been around much."

"No need to apologise, love." Adele smiled warmly, tilting her head as she noticed my hesitation. "Is something wrong?"

Everything. "*Nothing*."

"Savannah," Adele pushed, but her voice was gentle. "You can talk to us." She gestured between herself and Jason. "We're here."

"I know," I muttered, dragging in a long breath before glancing at the two of them. "I want to know *why*."

"Why what?" Adele tilted her head just as Jason took a curious step closer.

"Why you gave me up," I admitted quietly. "I'm not angry, but I think I deserve to know."

Jason sighed, looking at Adele for permission. She nodded right away, causing Jason to take a step closer. "We didn't want to give you up."

"You don't have to sugarcoat it," I cut in, realising how bitter my tone was. "I don't mean to be rude, but I can take it."

Jason nodded. "I know you can, Savannah. You're a strong girl. I don't doubt that you can handle it."

Adele put a hand up then, stopping his words. "We didn't mean to get pregnant, love."

My head snapped up at that.

"I was eighteen, and Adele was only sixteen," Jason continued to explain, smiling sadly at the memories. "We didn't find out until it was late in the pregnancy, and neither of us wanted to terminate."

"When we found out we were having twins, that only complicated it further," Adele stated with a sad breath. "A lovely family came to the hospital a few days before I gave birth, and they were interested in adopting one of our twins. They were happy to allow us visiting hours when you got older."

I laughed at the irony. "A lovely family."

"Savannah, dear. I am so deeply sorry," Adele said honestly. "If I had even the slightest idea that this family wouldn't love you right, we never would have gone through with it."

I didn't hesitate to say, "I know." Because I did. They weren't bad people. Just scared people.

"Those people were not your parents, Savannah," Jason said, hesitating as if he wasn't sure if it was the right thing to say. Still, he continued. "We always were, even if we were too afraid to show it then. We're here now."

"Do you see them?" I asked, worried. "In me? Do you see them in me?"

"Absolutely not." Adele was quick to comfort. "You don't have a Grey bone in your body."

I frowned, coming to a realisation. "I don't want to change my last name. I don't want to... feel further away from my brothers."

"You don't have to." Adele offered me a smile. "You don't have to do anything, love. This is all up to you."

"Okay," I whispered, more to myself than them. "I want to have a family," I admitted then, fiddling with my necklace. "It's just hard to accept it now."

"I know," Adele whispered soothingly. "But we'll be here when you're ready."

I nodded, rising from my seat. "Brooke's out tonight, but Theo's gonna stay over if that's okay?"

"Door stays open." Jason was quick to say.

Adele shook her head, huffing a laugh. "Door does not need to stay open."

Jason glanced at her. "Why not?"

"She said Theo." She glanced at her husband knowingly. "She didn't say Archie."

Jason let out a quick chuckle. "You're all good, then."

Was it that obvious?

God.

I walked back inside feeling both lighter and heavier somehow. Lighter, because I'd finally said it. Heavier, because it still didn't feel real. That kind of truth doesn't slot into your chest right away.

Once I made my way to my bedroom, Theo was already curled up on my bed like a cat.

"Are you gonna tell me why you really didn't wanna stay at Liv's tonight?" I asked, joining him on the bed. "Because I'm sure there's something bigger behind it."

"I just don't like the guy," he replied, not missing a beat. "I'm not one to judge, but Adam? The guy creeps me the fuck out."

I swallowed the lump in my throat, whispering, "I get that."

"Well, don't get soppy," he added, smirk returning.

I smiled a little, moving to my own bed as Theo tucked himself under the covers, readjusting the blanket five times until he was perfectly comfortable. It hit me then – how comfortable I was with him. Despite his weird, sarcastic energy, he was one of the very few people I'd always felt safe around.

I pulled my knees to my chest as I leant against the headboard, watching him grab the remote like he owned the place.

After a minute, he peeked up at me through his stupidly long lashes. "Okay, so are you gonna say it or do I have to drag it out of you?"

I blinked, rolling onto my left side so I could face him. "What?"

"You're in love with Archie," he stated, not a hint of uncertainty in his tone.

I rolled my eyes at his comment. "Don't start."

"Don't start?" He raised an eyebrow, resting his head on his elbow. "I've been bloody waiting for this moment."

I smiled, but didn't say anything.

"You're not denying it," he pointed out.

I stayed silent for a few moments, then whispered, "Because I can't."

"Why is it so complicated?"

"You're one to talk," I chuckled, shutting up when I realised how much I was projecting. "Okay. There's just a lot of… things. There's a lot to think about before anything happens between us again. Plus, I don't know what he wants."

Theo laughed. "That's because you're not in his head. I am, sort of. He never looked at anyone the way he looks at you."

I bit down on my lip. "Yeah. I don't—"

"I've known the guy forever, Sav," he interrupted. "The messy hookups, the random girls. And you know what? None of them meant anything. I never thought he'd find anybody he truly cared about." He shrugged. "Then *you* happened."

My throat tightened.

"I hope you know I wanna throw myself of a fucking bridge saying all this," he teased, only half-joking.

I knew that.

That's why it mattered more.

So, I laid back down, allowing my eyes to flutter closed.

Because Theo saw it too.

This *was* real.

FRIDAY WILL BE MAGICAL
SEPTEMBER 9TH 2004

SAVANNAH

"A school dance?" I repeated Liv's words, utterly confused. "That's an American thing, is it not?"

Liv nodded rapidly. She'd been practically bouncing on her toes since I showed up at her house this morning, which had only happened as she sent me an emergency text. The emergency being a school dance.

"I know," she agreed, grinning as she searched her wardrobe. "Isn't it exciting?"

"Mm hm," I laughed, impressed by this level of enthusiasm she never seemed to lose. It always came as a shock to me that one person could carry so much sunshine and joy, but I wasn't complaining. She'd always been my more sunny side.

"Okay, now, you should wear a blue dress," she informed me, pulling one out of her wardrobe. "What size are you?"

"Extra small," I said, then realised I'd put some weight on since living in a home that actually supplied food. "No, small."

Liv grinned in realisation, green eyes twinkling with joy as she placed the dress in my lap. "You have to wear this, then."

"Okay," I agreed with a laugh.

"I'm gonna wear this one," she announced, showing me this dress that I could only describe as the one Andie Anderson wore in how to lose a guy in ten days. It was... beautiful, to say the least.

"That's gorgeous." I nodded. "You definitely have to wear that. Since you're you, have you already made sure Theo's tie is yellow?"

"Of course I have," she responded, showing me the tie she bought for him. "It's the very same yellow, I made sure of it."

I laughed at her organization.

"Also," she continued, still searching her wardrobe like a madman. "I gave Archie a tie to wear, because, well, you're obviously going with him."

God. I hadn't even thought about that.

"Yeah. I'm going with him." Was my reply, because it only made sense. There certainly wasn't anybody else I'd be attending a dance with.

I still could hardly believe I was going to the dance at all, but it was making Liv happy. That's all that mattered.

As if she read my thoughts, Liv stopped rifling through her wardrobe just to beam at me. "You're gonna have a great time, I promise. I'm honestly still proud you didn't pretend to be deathly ill to get out of it."

"That was on the table," I snickered.

"It'll be so much fun," Liv argued, joining me on her bed. "You'll dance with your not-boyfriend who is certainly your boyfriend, we will all dance together, and then we eat all the food."

"*Theo* will eat all the food," I corrected, half-jokingly. Yeah, Theo didn't like to share food. He just liked to eat all of it.

Liv laughed at my words. "You're not wrong."

I grinned, holding the dress up to myself once more.

"Now, we only have eight days to prepare," Liv continued, looking panicked.

"Liv, eight days is a lot," I comforted, holding back a laugh as I rubbed her back. "I'm sure that's more than enough time."

"You're right," she agreed, jumping back up. "Friday will be magical."

DANCES AND OLD WARS
SEPTEMBER 17TH 2004

SAVANNAH

A few months ago, I couldn't have imagined myself in a silky, dark blue dress, surrounded by a sea of students at our school dance.

Yet, somehow, here I was.

My eyes darted around the room, searching for any familiar faces. And, I realised something. I had people to search for.

I used to wonder if I was wasting time. Like, if one day, I'd look back on my life and be disappointed in myself, you know? But I realised, I had my friends. I found safety. Hell, I found stability.

Regardless of the fact that my mind was an endless loop of thoughts, I was an entirely different girl to the start of the year.

I was beginning to think that was a good thing.

I caught a glimpse of Liv then. She was twirling around in that gorgeous yellow dress, and Theo, as always, was staring at her like she hung the stars. I couldn't remember a time where he hadn't looked at her like that.

And then, there was Archie.

The specific face I'd been looking for the entire night.

He was by the front stage, glancing around like he was searching for something. Over his white tuxedo, he wore a navy blue tie, thanks to Liv, of course.

The moment he caught my eye, he smiled. Not a smile of greeting, but one that said *there you are.*

I think that was the craziest part of it all. Not the fancy dress, not the school dance, not even the girl I'd become. But the fact that somebody could look at me like that and *mean* it.

That was one thing I was nearly certain wouldn't happen for me.

I truly didn't believe I'd get my happy ending.

But now? Well, the boy watching me from across the room wiped my doubt away every time I saw him.

So, I took a small step forward. Not a big one, but one that gave me hope. Hope that the girl I used to be, and the girl I was now, deserved this. Deserved to see what happened when I allowed myself to want something more than what I'd been handed.

I was finally becoming someone I didn't want to run away from.

"Hi." I smiled, cheeks flushing slightly as I approached the boy I'd spent this whole year falling in love with. "You look nice."

He smiled. "So do you."

I glanced down at myself, taking in my appearance. "Yeah, well, the makeup and fancy dress definitely do me well."

"You have always been beautiful," he protested, smiling warmly. He pushed himself off the wall he'd been leaning against, reaching to take my hand as Maroon 5's *She Will Be Loved* came on.

He glanced at me knowingly. "You love this song."

"I love this song," I confirmed with a quiet giggle, taking his hand. "Dance with me, Archie Bennett."

"Whatever you say." He grinned, following me onto the dance floor. His eyes darted around the room, looking confused. "They slow dance to this song? Really?"

"Hell yeah," I said, smiling sweetly. "Let's join them with that, huh?"

"Absolutely." He nodded, hand sliding down to my waist. His movements were careful, as if he wasn't sure if he was moving too fast.

I wrapped my arms around him, letting them rest on his upper back to show that I wasn't uncomfortable in the slightest. Actually, I couldn't remember a time where everything had felt so… right.

"This is our song," he declared, voice quiet, but loud enough for me to hear over the music. "I decided a few months ago."

"Didn't include me in the decision?" I teased, but I was smiling at his comment.

He shrugged happily, spinning me around slightly. "I'm still right."

"You're still right," I agreed, gently resting my head on his shoulder.

Whether he knew it or not, Archie was the only one who ever made me feel at home. I couldn't quite put my love for this boy into words, it was almost too much for me to carry. It was him. It was just *him*.

And I needed to act on those words soon.

We danced until the song came to an end, but as it did, we still stayed in place. The speakers began to blare some outgoing music then, but we continued dancing slowly. Neither of us really wanted to move.

I wasn't sure if I ever wanted to leave this moment. We had three grades of students in this one room tonight, but right now? It felt like we were the only two people around.

The fear I'd had when I first started falling for him wasn't entirely gone, but I was getting there. He made me feel like I was the moon, the stars, and the sun all at once. And I knew, if I screwed this up, there would be a long way to fall.

I just couldn't afford to ruin this.

Nothing had ever mattered as much as he did.

Instead of voicing anything, I smiled at him. A smile that told him everything I needed him to know.

Funnily enough, I was so deeply consumed by him. I saw it happen to Jayden. I saw it happen to

Liv. I even saw it happen to Izzie. Still, I never, in my wildest dreams, believed it could happen to me.

But it did.

Oh, it did.

I looked over Archie's shoulder, spotting Brooke from across the room. She was beside Liv, both of them dancing with different boys. Brooke was with the boy who looked through our window, and she looked happier than ever.

I still wasn't quite sure what she meant when she referred to him as her 'sometimes boyfriend', but, I don't think she knew either. All I saw was two people, deeply in love with the other.

Liv, of course, was in Theo's arms. Her blonde curls were in a loose bun, strands hanging out the front, with a shiny, silver headband on top.

I couldn't help but notice the way Theo's eyes never left hers. The two of them could deny it all they liked, but their relationship, however complicated it may have been, was built from deep love and mutual respect.

I'd always admired both of them for that.

Never thought I'd live it.

I looked back at Archie, gazing into those sharp, green eyes that softened around me. The eyes I'd learned to search for in a crowd full of people.

"You never ran from me," Archie stated as we swayed along to the music, smiling as he said it. "I'm really glad you never ran from me, Sav."

"I couldn't have," I admitted, voice soft and vulnerable. "You've always had some weird way of making me feel safe without even trying."

"Oh, I tried." Was his response, and I think it warmed something in my heart. Patched up the cracks that I thought had no chance at healing.

I grinned at his words, kissing him softly in front of everybody. I could feel people watching, but I didn't care. His lips moved against mine, and that was the only thing that mattered to me.

"I'm all in with you, Savannah Grey," he whispered once I pulled away, hand moving from my waist, and up to my cheek. "All in. Now and forever."

"Yeah?" I asked, eyes widening slightly. I think I needed to hear those words from him, even if I didn't know it.

I needed confirmation that he was as invested in this as I was.

Because I sure as hell was all in here.

"So am I," I added, feeling my expression soften. The crowd continued to talk, but he wasn't distracted. His eyes stayed unwavering on mine.

The moment was perfect.

That was, until I heard a shout from the hallway that could have only belonged to Izzie. She was the only one who could make those sounds. Those devastating sounds.

She was yelling at somebody, though, because her voice wasn't the only one I heard.

Peaking over Archie's shoulder once more, I saw that Liv and Theo were no longer on the dance floor.

That's when the worry kicked in like never before.

"We need to go," I said, but Archie was on it. He was already squeezing onto my hand, leading the way to the hall.

There was a sinking feeling in my stomach, and I knew, deep in my bones, that this wasn't going to be good.

Not. At. All.

We rushed through the glass doors, both pausing at the sight of Izzie and Theo, standing face to face, both with resigned expressions.

"What happened?" I desperately asked, eyes flicking to Liv, who was standing in the corner alone.

"I don't—I don't know." Liv shrugged, clearly worried as her eyes flickered between us and Theo. "She just started yelling."

"You still talk to him," Izzie demanded, tone sharper than a knife, but that didn't hide the tears streaming down her face. She hiccuped a sob, the tears making her look like a young child again. "I trusted you back then. I did. And you... you're friends with him."

"I'm not fuckling friends with that dick, Izzie!" Theo responded, his voice shaky at the end. He was pleading with her to believe him, but her eyes told me everything I needed to know.

Right now, she wasn't Izzie.

She was a dangerous, scared version of the girl I knew.

"Iz," Billy tried. He was the only person ever able to help her when she got like this, and I was counting on that piece of information now.

Instead of giving up, or talking to Billy, she stayed where she was, glaring at Theo like he was the enemy.

I wished I could have made her see that he wasn't.

"How can you do that?" Izzie choked out. "At least she doesn't know. You just..." She dropped her head to her hands, looking more miserable than ever. "You just let life go on when you *know* the truth."

Josie and Danny stepped in then, meaning every one of us was in this room. And I knew this was worse than usual.

This had to be the moment where all hell broke loose.

And nothing would ever be the same again.

"You're a fucking liar!" Izzie screamed at Theo, shoving him away from her when he tried to hug her.. "And you wonder why I can't even look at you."

"I don't even—"

"Do not," Izzie snapped, pointing a finger at him. Her hand was trembling, but she didn't let it show for very long. "Do not stand there and act like I'm fucking crazy. Everybody's been doing that since long before Marlee's death, and I can't fucking stand it!"

"What are you talking about, Izzie?" Danny asked, attempting to stand between them. Of course, that also earned him a shove toward the wall.

Izzie's eyes flickered back to Theo once her brother was out of the way. "You do not get to live your life and pretend you don't know what happened to her. What happened to all of us."

Theo's eyes darkened. "Fuck—"

"No!" Izzie screamed at the top of her lungs, shoving him further. "No. Do not fucking speak to me, Theo. You did this!"

Liv stepped between them, not bothering to hide any more. "Woah. Do not go there, Izzie! He did not do anything to Marlee. I get that you're angry-"

"You think I'm just angry?" Izzie scoffed, taking a step away from Theo, which, somehow, seemed more dangerous than pushing him. "I am devastated. My life has been over for a long time, and to push that further, my friend is dead."

"*Our* friend is dead," Liv corrected.

"Because of your own fucking brother!" Izzie shouted, voice more dangerous, more broken than I'd ever heard it.

Liv flinched, hands trembling.

Theo went quiet.

Actually, the entire room went quiet.

We all looked at Liv.

Liv and Billy were looking at Izzie.

Theo closed his eyes.

"You can't make these crazy accusations just because you're too afraid to face the truth," Liv stated, clearly afraid. "Marlee was sad, Izzie. There doesn't have to be a villain in that story."

"Maybe there didn't need to be one, but there is," Izzie argued. "And that villain lives with you."

Theo tried to speak, but his mouth instantly closed, like he knew anything he could say would only make it worse.

"Adam raped Marlee," Izzie continued, shaking her head like even telling this story broke her heart all over again. "He raped her. And I hope you all still think I'm fucking insane, but I truly doubt she was the only one." Her voice broke on the last few words, and everybody dropped to dead silence.

Billy was the first one to speak. "Iz." His voice was quiet and pleading, almost like he was begging her to stop, to walk away with him.

Izzie hesitated, but I visibly saw something break inside of her when she saw the hurt in Liv's eyes.

Izzie broke into sobs, running out of the hall. Billy followed after her immediately, leaving us here. Alone. With this.

Fuck.

I should have been the one to tell her.

Now...

This.

"She's crazy," Liv whispered, almost like she was trying to convince herself. She glanced up at me, then at Theo. "She's crazy, right? I mean, you *know* she's crazy."

"Adam did it." Was Theo's response, but he couldn't even look her in the eye. "She's not wrong, Livvy."

Liv's sobs started the moment those words left Theo's mouth, because she knew Theo would never lie to her.

"How can you possibly know that?" Liv begged, pulling on his arm.

"I just do," Theo replied, glancing around like he wasn't sure what he was supposed to say in this situation. "I just do."

"Fuck," Liv choked out, sobbing into her own arms.

Josie and Danny walked out immediately when Theo signaled for them to go, and he did the same for us.

I wasn't quite sure of what to do. Leaving Liv alone here after that reveal felt wrong on a million levels, but one glance at Theo was all it took for me to know she was in safe hands.

So, Archie and I walked out.

Walked away.

FIX YOU

SEPTEMBER 18TH 2004

ARCHIE

We'd been sitting on my balcony in silence for the past three hours.

Neither one of us had said a word.

Olivia looked fucking devastated earlier. Theo and Izzie clearly knew more than they led on. Danny was genuinely scared of his own sister. Billy was the savior, as always. Even Josie, who never liked to take things seriously, was petrified.

And Sav? She was holding a whole lot of guilt for one person.

She didn't deserve to feel guilty. I knew that. Deep down, she probably knew that too. But she still believed that she should have been strong enough to speak to Liv first so it didn't come out... well, the way it did.

Maybe that would have been better. It probably would have.

But that didn't mean Sav was at fault here.

"It's not your fault," I whispered, tightening my grip on her hand. Regardless of what she said, I knew that was what she needed to hear. "This is not your fault, Sav."

"I know that," she replied, tears drying up now. "I think I know that. I'm just… I should have told her, Archie."

I nodded. "Maybe. Maybe not. But we can't change the past, right?"

She offered me a weak smile, meeting my eyes for the first time since the reveal. "Izzie looked really scared, Archie."

"I know," I agreed, voice quiet enough for comfort, but loud enough for her to know I meant what I said. "Everyone looked scared."

"No." She shook her head. "No, Archie. She looked *really* scared."

I blew out a shaky breath, knowing she was right. I'd never seen anybody look so terrified, angry, and miserable all at once, let alone Izzie Harris. "She did."

"It's probably soon to bring it up," I started, calculating how the best way to say this was. "But… Liv knows now. If you want to do anything about Adam, that might need to happen soon."

"I know," she agreed with a half-smile. "Maybe I can go visit Lila tomorrow."

"Marlee's mum?" I asked, proud of her strength. Screw that, I was always proud of her strength. Savannah Grey was a bloody soldier.

"Yeah," she confirmed with a small, sweet nod. "She deserves to know."

"More than anybody," I whispered.

Mum joined us on the balcony then, a worried frown etched into her face. "How are you doing, Savannah?"

"I'm okay, Mrs. Bennett."

"Carrie," Mum corrected with a smile, taking a seat beside Sav. "Archer mentioned you might want to take this to court?"

Sav nodded. "If Marlee's Mum agrees."

"Okay," Mum replied, voice warmer than usual, like maybe she knew exactly what Sav needed. "Well, I wanted you to know that I'll be here when you know what you want to do. I have connections."

Sav laughed at her words, but she sounded genuinely grateful. "Thank you, Mrs—" She paused, remembering what Mum said. "Thank you, Carrie. So much."

"Anytime, love." Mum nodded, rising from her seat. "I'll let you two chat. But if either of you have any questions, I'll be right here."

"Thank you," Sav and I said in unison, just as Mum headed back inside.

"See that?" I asked, nudging her shoulder slightly. "We've got a good chance."

"I want to be with you," she suddenly blurted out, turning her body to face me. "It's random, and maybe it's bad timing, but it's true. God, Archie, it's so true. I just want you. Forever."

"Are you proposing to me?" I attempted to tease, but I couldn't hide the soft affection in my voice as I pulled her in closer. "Joking. I think it's been clear since day one that you're the only one for me, Sav."

"So…" She started, biting down on her lip. "Then be my real boyfriend."

"Your real boyfriend," I snickered, chuckling softly.

But then I caught a glimpse of vulnerability in her eyes, and realised all she needed to hear from me was yes for her to feel whole again.

I would have learned how to fly a goddamn spaceship for the girl. If all she needed was one word, I would happily give her that.

"Of course." I grinned, tucking a loose strand of hair back behind her ear. "Yeah."

Her smile widened, and she pressed her lips to mine, tender, yet passionate.

I pulled back to whisper against her lips, "Whatever happens next, we can do it."

She nodded in agreement, tugging me closer, almost as if she needed me like air. "We can."

Sav deepened the kiss once more, and I could feel her smile against my lips. "We'll be okay."

That's when I heard the knock.

SAVANNAH

I offered Archie a small smile as I rose from the couch. "Stay here. I'll get it."

"Thanks."

Making my way towards the front door, I went over every detail in my head.

It was late.

Nobody came knocking at this time.

Worried, I peeked through the peephole. When I saw Izzie on the porch—face blotchy, hair tangled, sleeves pulled down—that worry only spread further. It mixed with something that felt a lot like fear.

As I opened the door, a weak smile appeared on her face. "I tried your house. Adele said you were here and I—" She blew out a tired breath. "I didn't know where else to go."

I didn't hesitate to let her inside. "You're always welcome, Izzie. No matter where I am, or how screwed up things are."

She nodded gratefully, closing the door behind herself. "Can we talk?"

I paused for a moment, studying her blue eyes. After a few seconds – I could tell she needed it. Because she came to me. Izzie Harris didn't ask for help unless she was breaking.

And I wouldn't stand by and let her collapse.

Shooting a glance at Archie, he saw the state of Izzie and didn't hesitate to nod.

Thankful, I took her hand and directed her to Archie's bedroom upstairs.

For a while, there was silence – thick and stretching.

Then, "I think I broke something again."

I shook my head, agreeing with her. "No. You told the truth, okay? You said the right thing."

"But nobody wanted to hear it," Izzie replied, wrapping her arms protectively around herself. "They looked at me like I was insane, Sav. They've *always* looked at me like I'm insane."

"You're not," I said softly.

"Sometimes, I feel like I am," she admitted with a helpless shrug. "I mean... I lost everyone, Sav. Everything."

"Not me," I reminded her with a weak smile.

"Not you," she agreed. "But I just can't... I'm so angry. Always. It just—" She pressed her palms to her eyes, drying the tears before they had a chance to fall. "It always comes out like fire."

I didn't offer what I would to somebody—anybody—else.

Because this was Izzie.

She didn't need to hear *It'll be okay*, because she was well aware that it wouldn't. Not now, anyway. She didn't need me to pretend everything was normal.

Instead, I wrapped my arms around her. For a moment, she struggled. Then, I felt her body loosen up as she let herself collapse into my arms.

"I'm glad you did it," I told her honestly. "And if you didn't, I would have. Liv will come around. Everybody will – because this is about Marlee. So, yeah. You did the right thing, even if it was hard."

"I'm scared," Izzie admitted – and it was insane, because I'd never heard those words from her mouth before.

"So am I," I whispered back. "But aren't we all a little scared sometimes?"

"Sometimes."

Another beat of silence.

Then, Izzie whispered, "You don't think I'm a monster?"

"No," I answered without hesitation. "I think you're the bravest person I've ever known."

"I think I'm gonna cry," Izzie said, sounding disgusted. "If I cry, you can never tell anybody about it."

"Okay," I replied with a small laugh. "I promise."

"Thank you," Izzie replied, and there it was.

The gut-wrenching sobs I'd been waiting to hear for far too many years.

The tears she never believed she could cry.

ECHOES OF OLD FRIENDS
SEPTEMBER 19TH 2004

SAVANNAH

I'd been conflicted all morning.

Speaking to Lila McGovern felt like a death sentence and a lifeline all at once, and I had no idea what the outcome would be.

I mean, back when we hung out at Marlee's house all the time, she was a wonderful person.

But grief changes people, and I could only hope that she was the same woman I used to know.

Regardless of the fear rushing through my veins, I forced myself to show up at an achingly familiar front porch. One that I hadn't stepped foot on since Marlee's death.

The flowers that once hung over the doorway were gone, and through the window, I could already count three photos of Marlee hanging on the walls.

The walls were painted. It was a subtle difference of cream shades, but it happened.

Without the support of Archie and Carrie, I wasn't sure if I could have shown up today. This was a huge step, and I probably wasn't ready in the slightest.

I still wasn't sure if Liv believed what Izzie told her, and I knew nobody else would be in the right headspace to hear about this, but it needed to be done anyway.

Blowing out a shaky breath, I reached my hand out, and gently knocked on the door I'd spent so many summers opening when I was little.

God, I needed to keep it together.

I wasn't the one getting horrific news here, but it sure felt like it.

The door flew open, revealing a version of Lila that was almost unrecognizable. When Marlee was alive, she wore blonde extensions. Now? Her natural hair was back, a chaotic mess of tangled brown curls.

She still looked pretty, just... a bit lifeless.

I didn't blame her, but at the same time, it broke my heart a little bit. Seeing her like this. Knowing what she was about to find out would break her all over again.

But keeping it from her would make it so much worse.

And this time? I needed to be strong.

"Hi, dear." Lila squinted as if she was trying to recognise me. A few seconds later, her face regained some colour, and she smiled kindly. "Little Savannah Grey."

I offered her an awkward smile. "Hi, Lila."

"Oh, you have grown so much," she stated, eyes widening as she looked at me. "You look so much happier."

"My parents died," I admitted, word vomit spilling all over the place. Yeah, that wasn't a good nervous trait of mine. "They weren't very good."

"I remember," Lila replied, smiling at my words. "Well, I haven't seen you in forever."

Her words hit me like a train.

Shit. Not an appropriate comparison.

Keep it together, Savannah!

"I know, I'm sorry," I whispered, offering her a weak smile. "I should have come around more. I'm so, so sorry."

"Don't be silly," she answered, stepping aside. She gestured for me to come in, a smile still etched onto her face. "Nobody came around again. I didn't expect anyone to."

I nodded. "Still. I should have been stronger. It must be… really hard for you."

"It certainly hasn't been easy," she honestly admitted, flicking the kettle on. "Would you like a drink?"

I shook my head, then nodded. "A coffee would be great."

She looked at me like I was crazy to be drinking coffee at five pm, but she began making it anyway.

I mean, it probably was crazy, but caffeine helped with my nerves.

Honestly, I would have taken wine if she offered it to me, and I hated wine. I hadn't felt this sickly anxious in years, and I didn't appreciate the feeling.

"Where's Deacon?" I asked, eyes darting around the room. I couldn't see her husband anywhere, and the last time I checked, he still worked from home.

"Oh." Lila frowned, but quickly recovered. "We got a divorce."

My hand moved to cover my mouth. Christ, this poor woman.

"I am so sorry," I told her, feeling a deep surge of sympathy for Lila McGovern. She'd been through enough to last four lifetimes. "I had no idea."

"Well, that's okay." She nodded, placing my coffee in front of me before she joined me at the dining table. "We got divorced a few months after... after Marlee died. I suppose it showed us what mattered most, and we needed to be apart. It was for the best."

"Okay," I said quietly, sipping my coffee. Anything to stop me from speaking.

She seemed so excited that somebody finally showed up to see her, and I didn't want to ruin that too quickly.

I didn't want to ruin it at all, but I knew I had to.

"What brought you here today?" she asked with a smile, a dagger through my chest.

"I've been thinking about you a lot. Just thought I'd come visit," I lied through my teeth, feeling a strong need to comfort her before breaking her heart a little more.

She smiled at my words, taking a sip of her tea. "I think about you guys every day."

"Yeah?"

She nodded her head in confirmation. "Especially you and Izzie. How is she doing?"

I hesitated before saying, "Not so great."

"Oh." She shook her head sadly. "Did the bipolar worsen with age? I was so worried when the poor baby got diagnosed back then, but I hoped it would fade with time, even though it's impossible."

"Ah. I suppose, that and the grief," I informed, voice barely above a whisper as I scanned the walls. The photos of Marlee hit me hard, and brought me back to the days when she was alive. Even though they were some of the worst times of my life, it didn't matter. Because she was alive. "She's trying to stay strong, though."

"She was always a strong one," Lila agreed, then squinted. "Savannah," she whispered knowingly.

My head snapped up. "Yes?"

"What really brought you here?" she asked, stopping me as I tried to speak again. "I know it wasn't just because you were thinking about me."

I nodded, confirming her words. "Yeah, there's more to it."

"Okay," she whispered, hands trembling around her mug. "What do you know, Savannah? I am dying here," she admitted, tears welling up in her eyes. "What do you know about my baby?"

Her words cut through to my soul, and I immediately passed her the letter.

She wasted no time before opening it, and I watched her every expression as she read through the lines.

By the middle, the tears were falling freely, and I was stuck in place. I didn't know if I was supposed to speak, or comfort her, or do nothing. So, I waited.

Once she read the last line, she glanced up at me, lips trembling as she tried and failed to speak. "Is this… this is from Marlee?" she finally asked.

"Yes," I confirmed, taking the letter as she passed it back. "I'm sorry."

"I will be taking this to court, Savannah," she told me.

"I hoped you would be," I replied, finally pulling her into a tight embrace. "I am so sorry, Lila."

"Thank you," she whispered into my hair. "Thank you so much for telling me."

"Of course."

"I want you all to be present in court," she said, but it sounded more like a question. "Since our law is different, you're all valid to show up as witnesses."

"Okay," I agreed without hesitation. "I'm happy to do that, and I'll get the others on board. Don't worry."

"All I do now is worry, Savannah," she whispered with a sad smile. "At least, now, I know why my baby left me."

I swallowed the lump in my throat, heart aching at her words.

God, she just wanted her child back.

Somehow, I'd been able to get everybody to agree to meet at my house. I hadn't given much information, but in each call, I included that I went to Lila's house, so it wasn't like they were walking into this completely blind.

Archie may not have been involved in the case at all, but he was the first person I invited. I knew I wouldn't be able to handle this on my own.

Judging from how things went down at the dance, Liv would still be heartbroken and afraid, Theo would be worried, and there was no saying how Izzie was going to react.

But I had to hold onto the hope that they'd all be on board. Without them, this case wouldn't go forward the same.

I figured Marlee deserved at least this.

Even if it was hard for them, which I understood, we needed to do this for our friend. I don't think I could have lived with myself if we didn't.

Archie, of course, was the first one to arrive.

He was sitting beside me on the dining table, six empty seats surrounding it, preparing for whatever came next.

I'd be lying if I said I wasn't nervous to tell everybody. The truth was, it was terrifying. I had no idea how they'd react, or how they'd be feeling, and that only made it worse.

Because this was all about chance.

And Marlee's memory deserved more than the flip of a coin.

A few moments later, Josie strolled in. "Hi." She smiled, auburn hair slicked back into a braid. "Are you guys okay?"

I nodded, offering her a smile to lighten the mood. I gestured for her to take a seat, keeping my face as enthusiastic as possible so this didn't feel like a press conference. "Yeah. We just have to wait for the others."

Right on cue, Theo and Liv came in, Izzie and Billy following shortly behind.

"Hi," Theo said, the only one to even glance up as they all walked in.

Liv spotted me, and I could see her expression soften as she did. "Hi, Savannah."

I smiled at her, gesturing for her to sit. "Hi, Liv."

Everybody took their seats, and despite my best efforts, it sure felt a whole lot like a press conference.

"Okay." I nodded, blowing out a shaky breath. I needed to prepare myself for the worst, and hope for the best. "It's about Marlee," I admitted, deciding to give them some context.

Izzie made a move to get up, but Billy gently tugged her arm, keeping her in place. She huffed a breath, gesturing for me to continue.

"I visited Lila, and… I showed her Marlee's letter," I informed them, biting down on my lip. I almost wanted to squeeze my eyes closed and will myself somewhere else, but I knew I needed to stay present.

To my surprise, they all nodded along. Including Izzie and Liv.

"She, um…" I trailed off, deciding the best way to put this into words. "She wants to take it to court."

Theo's eyes widened, clearly shocked, but he quickly returned back to normal, hooking an arm over Liv's shoulder. "She does?"

I nodded, dragging in a long breath. I felt Archie's grip tighten on my hand, and that was enough reassurance for me to continue. "She does. And she wants us to be there as witnesses."

"Okay, none of us witnessed this," Danny said, raising an eyebrow. "How does that even work?"

I shrugged, because that was all I could do. "I don't know. Our town is weird."

"That's for sure," Billy spoke, tilting his head slightly. "So they want all of us to testify against him?"

"Yeah," I whispered.

"Only about Marlee?" he asked, confusing me further.

"Of course." I frowned, searching his eyes, but there was nothing to be found. "Yeah, only Marlee."

"But everyone needs to consent for this to go through," Archie explained, clearly noticing the tremble in my hands.

"I'll do it," Danny and Josie said in unison. "He deserves to be locked up forever if he did that to Marlee," Josie continued. "It's a no-brainer if you ask me."

Izzie shook her head before nodding. "Okay," she whispered, voice hardly audible. "I can do it," she added, voice breaking.

Billy smiled proudly, but it faded just as quickly. "Yeah, I'm in." He nodded, eyes darting to Liv and Theo, the only two who hadn't given their input yet.

"Guys?" Archie whispered, hopefulness clear in his voice.

Theo took one look at Liv, then back at me. "I don't know if I can do that."

"I can," Liv said, not meeting anyone's eyes. "But I'm not gonna stand there and lie. He's my brother, and I had no clue about any of this. I can't say I had any suspicions."

"You don't believe her?" Theo asked, looking personally hurt.

"Of *course* I believe her," Liv cleared up. "And I'll say that. But I mean, I can't pretend I knew any of this was happening."

Theo sighed, meeting my eyes, looking conflicted. "Alright, then. I'm in."

I blew out a sigh of relief, thankful I didn't need to convince them much.

They were in.

Which meant we were doing this.

Really doing this.

Archie squeezed my hand firmer, leaning in to whisper in my ear, "We can do this."

Izzie stood suddenly, a mix of anger and relief washing over her face. "I have to get to music class," she announced.

"Music?" I frowned, feeling like I didn't know my friend at all. "You do music?"

Now she just looked upset. "I've always done music," she whispered before quickly regaining her composure. "I guess Marlee was right." She offered a soft laugh as she approached the front door, glancing over her shoulder. "I am mysterious."

That she was.

Izzie Harris was a puzzle everybody was afraid to solve.

OUR TABLE NEVER CHANGED

SEPTEMBER 20TH 2004

ARCHIE

School was more fucking awkward than ever.

We were all sitting at our usual table, as if nothing had changed at all. Except, *everything* had changed.

There had to be more to the story. Deep down, I knew that.

But something inside of me stopped me from voicing those concerns, and chose to keep it inside. It felt selfish being the one to raise those ideas when I shouldn't have even been involved in this.

I wasn't. Not really.

I was just sticking around because I knew Sav needed me. I knew she did, because she kept asking me to stay when they talked about the court stuff, about Marlee.

Savannah Grey was a lot of things, but she wasn't someone who admitted to needing help. Not unless she really did.

I wasn't sure what I could do for her, but she told me a million times that being there was enough. So, I kept doing that, and I knew I'd never stop.

It was Sav, after all.

As unexpected as it was, she was the only one I'd ever wanted around. The only person in the entire fucking universe that had managed to pull true feelings out of me.

It was both amazing and depressing all at once.

"We still don't have any updates?" Izzie asked from the other end of the table, glancing at me. "Didn't your Mum say she could make sure this process was fast?"

I nodded. "Yeah, but not one-day fast."

Izzie sighed, leaning back in her chair. Somehow, her dark blue eyes weren't filled with the bitterness they'd carried for years. She just looked scared. Like the rest of us.

God, I knew Theo hated the girl, and she'd given him every reason to, but it was nearly fucking impossible to hate her when she showed she was capable of goodness.

"Carrie said we should know something by Wednesday at the latest," Sav explained, taking the words from my mouth before I was forced to say them.

"Okay," Liv and Josie said in unison, looking relieved that we at least knew that.

I caught a glimpse of Mason Capiel approaching the table then, looking every bit as smug and fucking stupid as he was. "Who's this one?" he asked, grinning down at Sav, who moved closer to me.

"My girlfriend, Capiel," I said, but the look in my eyes told him it was a warning. Still, I decided to make it clear. "My girlfriend that you'll stay the fuck away from."

He took a step back, clearly embarrassed. "Jesus. Sorry, Cap."

"Yeah, go on, now." I narrowed my eyes, chuckling once he walked away.

I never understood it.

I wasn't scary, but the guys on my team seemed to think the very opposite. It was fucking hilarious.

"I don't like that." Sav frowned. "Does being your girlfriend really come with a million guys asking about me?"

"Unfortunately," I answered with a dramatic sigh. "Don't worry, though. Not all of them will be hitting on you."

She laughed slightly, turning her attention back to the group, who were just as tense as they had been since Sav told them. It was bloody awful, to say the least.

Josie picked at the label on her water bottle, and Theo kept an arm casually draped over Liv's seat, like usual, except I could see the way his jaw tensed anytime someone spoke.

"We'll know something soon," I said, deciding to break the silence. "That's something."

They all nodded in unison.

It wasn't much, and it was a very complicated situation, but we had to stay strong. No, I needed to stay strong. For them. For Sav.

ANYONE BUT YOU

SEPTEMBER 22ND 2004

SAVANNAH

Archie and I had been sitting on the clifftop for the past half an hour, desperately awaiting a call.

I knew there was a chance it would be late. Carrie did warn us that it could take a few weeks if the case was very complicated, or if they found more evidence.

But I was still holding onto hope that it would come today.

I fiddled with my necklace, subtly watching Archie out of the corner of my eye. He wasn't speaking, just watching the stars ahead like they could fix this.

"I don't wanna drag you down with me," I blurted out, voice quiet. Nervous.

His head snapped up, eyes locking on mine. "What do you mean?"

"It's a lot." I shrugged. "Marlee. The court. My past." I smiled understandingly at him, the fear of hurting him digging at my ribs. "I don't want you to feel the need to stick around."

"Sav, I've been telling you since day one," he insisted, sliding closer to me. "I am not going anywhere."

"I know, I just…" I trailed off, finally looking into his eyes again. "One day, in the future, I don't want you to resent me because I kept you from… I don't know. Everything."

"You *give* me everything," he argued, violently shaking his head. "And you don't get to walk away from me."

I smiled sadly. "I'm not going to. I'm just giving you the option if you wanna take it."

"Well, I don't," he responded without hesitation, tilting my chin up. "It's never not been you," he whispered. "It's never been anyone but you."

I chuckled at his words. "Don't flatter me, now. All those other girls…"

"None of those other girls mattered, Sav. Not then, and definitely not now," he said, smiling down at me. "But you do. You matter."

"Yeah?" I whispered, smiling as his hand slid to my cheek.

"Yeah," he confirmed with a small nod. "And I'll keep telling you that until I'm certain you believe me."

I huffed a laugh. "Thank you for telling me."

He grinned, hand resting on my cheek still. "Always."

He moved to kiss me just as his phone vibrated on his pocket, causing both of us to jump.

"Answer it," I instructed, pointing to his phone. "Quick!"

"Okay, okay." He blew out a nervous breath, then pressed answer. He moved the phone to his ear, biting down on his lip as his mum spoke.

"Yeah," he whispered in response to something she said, but I couldn't tell what it was. "Okay. No, that's great. Yeah. Really? Alright. Thank you."

He hung up the phone then, tucking it into his pocket before glancing at me. For the first time in a while, there was close to no emotion in his expression, and it was killing me trying to read through the lines.

"Yes or no?" I asked, nervously fiddling with my fingers.

He nodded firmly. "Yeah. We're doing this. Court dates aren't fully decided, but sometime in the next three weeks."

I smiled, unsure of how to feel. Obviously, we were going to court for a disgusting reason, but this may have been our only chance at helping Marlee get justice.

And I was utterly thankful we had that chance.

"That's really good," I whispered, nodding rapidly. "So good."

Archie reached for my hand again, weaving his fingers through mine like it grounded him. Like it grounded *us*.

I smiled, fighting back the sting in my eyes. I hated crying. Especially now.

Of course, he noticed. He pulled me into a tight hug, giving me more comfort than anybody else possibly could. "Are you okay?"

I nodded against his hair. "I am. Just have to survive the next few weeks."

"You will." He pulled back, pressing a soft kiss to my forehead. "And I'll be here every step of the way."

God. Sometimes I didn't even know what to do with the way he said things. Like he believed it more than I ever could. Like he saw the future I couldn't let myself picture yet.

In all honesty, I could hardly picture a life for myself. When I closed my eyes, I couldn't see further than next year. I was too afraid to want more if that meant I could lose it.

Archie stepped back, draping his jacket over my shoulders. "Why don't we get you home?" he asked, tilting his head slightly.

Home.

That word wasn't a lie anymore.

"Okay," I agreed, nodding my head. "That's a good idea." Before hopping into his car, I stopped in my tracks. "You will be at the court when it happens, right?"

He nodded without hesitation. "Of course I will. I told you, I'm here for all of it."

I jumped into his car, mind flashing back to the first time I'd been in here. Yeah, that was awkward as hell.

"How many times did you meet Marlee?" I asked, suddenly curious about his experience with her. I knew he hadn't been close with her, but he'd definitely spoken to her here and there.

"Only a few," he said, turning on the engine. He thought for a moment, tapping his finger against his chin, then said, "But I remember when Theo insisted we included her in Primary school."

I laughed, impressed. "Wow. Theo being the peacemaker."

"Nah." He shook his head, huffing a chuckle. "He just wanted us to let Liv play, and he included Marlee to make it seem casual."

"Theo always played with Liv," I agreed, laughing. I hadn't gone to Primary School with them, but I still hung out with them every chance I got. They were my safe place back then.

"He did," Archie agreed. "He got fucking bullied for it, but it was definitely sweet."

"Always loved her, huh?"

"Blatantly obvious," he agreed with a smirk. "Hopefully they act on it one day."

"Marlee was always the biggest supporter of Liv and Theo." I smiled at the memories, tilting my head simply to watch Archie as he drove. "She probably wrote songs about their relationship."

He chuckled. "I could see that happening."

"She would have been front row at their wedding." I picked at my nails, subconsciously allowing the grief back in.

No, bad idea, Sav.

"Don't do it," Archie whispered, clearly catching on. He reached his other hand across to hold mine, warm and steady. "Once you let those feelings in, they take forever to leave."

"Doesn't stop, does it?" I bit down on my lip, desperately needing that answer from somebody who had also been here under different circumstances.

"Not really," he said honestly, squeezing on my hand. "But it slows."

"Yeah?" I asked, head snapping up.

"Yeah," he confirmed quietly, smiling lovingly at me. "It slows."

"I hope so," I laughed softly. "Kinda feels like I'm being stabbed when I think about her."

"I get that," Archie answered, making a sharp turn toward my house. "Hey, let's hang out after school tomorrow?"

I nodded in agreement, then frowned. "Don't you have training?"

"Yeah, but we finish at five on Thursday's," he explained, parking in front of my house. "So we can hang out after that."

"Okay," I agreed, stepping out of his car. "Thank you."

"Of course." He grinned, shooting me a wink. "I'll be seeing you!"

I laughed, throwing my head back and shooting him a wave over my head.

Yeah, I was screwed.

And I wasn't complaining.

MY BEST GUY

SEPTEMBER 23RD 2004

ARCHIE

"Alright, boys!" Coach called from the sidelines, grinning to himself. "Basketball season is finally back."

I smiled, throwing my last ball of the day through the hoop, not missing a beat.

Danny was the only guy on the team I didn't wanna smash over the head with a fucking hammer that showed up today.

Billy and Theo both took the day off.

I understood it, but it was shit without them here.

In all honesty, I didn't need these training sessions. And, yeah, that was definitely cocky of me. But even now, with all the time I'd taken off, I was still the best guy on the team.

I didn't see that changing.

Coach already told me there were five professional teams wanting me on them once I finished school, so I wasn't too worried.

Spending my entire life with a ball in my hand definitely paid off.

I headed over to where Coach stood by the empty bleachers, smiling as I approached him. "Hey, Coach."

"My best guy." His brown eyes lit up with satisfaction. "Don't tell 'em, but the team is shit every time you're away."

I chuckled at his words, joining him as he sat on the bench.

"My birthday was yesterday," he muttered, wrinkles deepening as he frowned. "I sat at my wife's grave all day."

His words hit me like a truck. I didn't want to imagine Coach sad. The guy was like a dad to me. "I'm sorry."

"Ah, that's okay, kid," he assured me, smiling fondly. "Just wanted to know you weren't the only one with that empty void on your birthday."

I swallowed hard, wondering how he knew that when I'd barely even allowed myself to remember.

"Takes one to know one," he explained, voice soft and knowing. "But I'm right here. You can jump off that high-horse with not wanting me as a father figure any time ya like, because, like it or not, I already am."

I laughed at his confidence, and stopped because he was right. "Yeah. You already are."

"How's it going with the girl?" he continued poking in my life, but I didn't mind. No, he'd earned the rights a long time ago.

"Good," I answered. "Lots of shit going on, but she's doing better than she was last year."

He nodded, the look in his eyes telling me he'd heard about Sav's family. I wasn't surprised, considering everyone and their mothers knew the day after they died.

"I taught Michael Grey," Coach explained, shaking his head at the memories. "Always knew he wasn't a good guy. Never in my life thought he would be a father."

"No?" I asked, interested in what he knew.

"Nope," he said, frowning as he glanced at me. "He was pretty bloody violent. It was high school, so no one looked further into it." He sighed before adding, "I truly wish we had."

I nodded along as he spoke, soaking up this new information. It made sense. A guy like Michael Grey? One that could be so violent toward people he was supposed to love? There was no way that randomly started one day.

It must have been deeply rooted in his veins.

"I'm glad she's doing better," he told me, lightening the mood. "Savannah Grey is a very bright girl, son. She will go far."

"She certainly will, Coach," I agreed with a firm nod. "No doubts there."

"You all prepared for court?" he questioned me, squinting slightly. "Not an easy position to be in."

"How do you know *everything*?" I chuckled, genuinely impressed.

Ever since my dad and Elsie died, Coach Holloway had seemed to know more about me than I did myself, almost like he watched out for me. Screw that, he did watch out for me. I knew he did.

"Don't give up on her, son." Was his straightforward answer. "She needed somebody like you in her life."

I smiled at his words, but hid it behind another nod. "Thanks, Coach." I checked my phone, realising the time. "I have to go, alright? Meeting up with Sav."

"You do that, kid." He shot me a wink as I stood. "I'll see ya."

✦

"Hi." I grinned once I reached Sav's room. She was sitting cross-legged on her bed, watching some sad movie on TV as I joined her.

"Hey." Her entire face lit up once she saw me. She grabbed the remote, immediately shutting the TV down and giving me her full attention. "How was training?"

"Good," I said with a sigh, making myself comfortable in her bed. "Fucking exhausting, though."

"Mm," she hummed in agreement, clearly thinking about something else.

"What's on that mind of yours?" I asked, tilting my head in curiosity.

"I should go back to cheer sometime," she told me, frowning at the idea. "Liv's been out, and I don't wanna fail the team by staying home."

"Nah, don't worry," I insisted, wrapping an arm over her shoulder. "Coach has it all under control, anyway. You'll go back when you're ready to go back."

She smiled at my words. "You're like superman."

"What?" My head snapped up as I chuckled at her words.

She palmed her hand over her face, clearly embarrassed by her statement. "I'm sorry. I'm not good at the talking thing."

I chuckled, leaning my head against her pillow. "You're doing just fine."

"Maybe. I think I've forgotten how to just… be," she admitted, sighing thoughtfully. "It's like the moment everything's calm, I'm waiting for it to blow up."

My chest tightened. "Because you're used to being in survival mode all the time. It's not bad, just a habit that hasn't been broken yet."

She looked down at our hands, where her thumb was now tracing lazy patterns on my hand. "That's not fair to you."

"Don't say that," I immediately responded.

"But it's true. You're kind and patient and good. But me?" She paused, letting out a short, bitter laugh. "I'm like a fire that never stops burning."

"Then I'll breathe in the smoke," I replied easily, shaking my head. "I didn't go into this blind."

That caught her attention. Her eyes locked on mine, wide and vulnerable. "Why stay?"

"Because losing you would mean losing the only thing that ever felt real." I shrugged. "I don't wanna live to see the day where that happens."

She smiled at that.

"And you're not just a burning fire," I told her, desperate to make her see herself the way I did. The way everybody else did. "You are clever and sweet and loyal. I never doubted that."

"You didn't?" she asked.

"I never doubted you," I confirmed with a comforting smile, then frowned. "Plus, I'm not the only one that sees that. I wish it wasn't true, but half the guys at school would jump at the chance of being with you."

That got her laughing. "Lucky I don't want any of them, huh?"

"So fucking lucky," I agreed.

"I used to think I wouldn't make it to sixteen, let alone further," she murmured a few moments later, head now resting against my chest.

My hand froze in her hair.

"I didn't mean it in a dramatic way," she added, as if she felt bad for dropping something so heavy. "It just never felt like I'd live a normal life, you know?"

My arms tightened around her without even thinking. "You're doing that now, Sav."

"I know," she said in agreement. Then she whispered, "If I mess this up, will you hate me?"

I sat up just enough to look her in the eye, firm but loving. "No. I will *never* hate you."

She sighed. "You say that now."

"No," I shook my head, unwavering. "I say that because I mean it. You don't scare me, Sav. Not even when you try to."

"I'm terrified," she admitted, and I could see the tears welling up in her grey eyes. "Of the trial. Of messing this up with you. Of waking up one day and realising it was all a dream, realising I'm actually still stuck in that house."

"You are not stuck," I insisted fiercely. "You're not stuck anymore."

She leaned in and kissed me then, hand trembling on my cheek like she was holding on with everything she had.

And I let her.

Because she wasn't just my girl. She was the *whole damn story.*

NO BODY, NO CRIME

OCTOBER 9TH 2004

SAVANNAH

This was it.

The day where Marlee's story either fell into place, or broke into even more pieces. Ones that couldn't be put back together.

And I felt like throwing up.

Marlee's mother had testified earlier this morning, and we hadn't been needed for that part.

But, they had decided on an order when we first showed up an hour ago. Josie would testify first, then Danny and Theo. We'd get a recess after that, then I would have to testify.

With Adam across the room.

God, it was horrifying.

But every time it felt like too much, I remembered what Marlee had to experience, and I knew I needed to continue.

After me, only Izzie, Liv, and Billy would be left to testify.

I wasn't sure how I'd survive my own testimony as well as each one of my friends, but I needed to do it.

When the judge called her name, Josie stepped up to the witness stand as if she had nothing more to lose.

She sat down, adjusted the microphone to her height, and when they asked if she was ready to begin, she purposely glared right at Adam. Her attention then shifted to the jury as she said, "She was thirteen. I need you to understand that before I continue. Marlee McGovern was thirteen when this mons—" She cleared her throat, regaining her composure. "She was thirteen when this… incident occured."

She took a moment of silence, letting that number sink in. making sure everybody understood how young that really was.

"I used to think he was charming," she continued, voice strong and steady. "Everyone did, actually. That's how guys like him get away with terrible things." She narrowed her eyes, making sure the jury understood. "Just like Ted Bundy."

Josie took a breath.

"I wish we had noticed sooner, but we didn't," she announced. "But I remember when it happened. I remember when she stopped eating. Stopped sleeping. Stopped being Marlee."

She leaned back in her chair, stronger than ever before. Her eyes moved back to where Adam sat, staring at him with this unwavering anger. "Marlee McGovern did not lie. Her truth is right in front of you all."

Josie looked down at her feet, then back up at the room. "That's all," she finished, returning to the seats where we were.

Jesus.

I wasn't sure if I could get up there and speak as strongly as she did, but I knew I needed to. Because one speech made all the difference here.

After a minute, Danny stepped up to the stand without a single hint of hesitation. "I knew Marlee for a very, very long time. She was a good friend of mine," he explained, eyes flicking between Adam and the jury.

A pause.

Just one.

"Marlee didn't tell anyone," Danny continued, eyes locked on Adam now. "Not until she killed herself. Let that sink in," he announced, voice breaking subtly. "She did not tell anybody until it was too late. Until she was writing her suicide notes. A thirteen year old girl shouldn't be writing suicide notes, let alone explaining the rape she endured at the hands of a man she trusted."

Izzie wiped her eyes from beside me, trying and failing to hide her fear.

Theo and Liv looked afraid as much as they did miserable.

Billy was attempting to stay strong for them, but I could see the tremble in his hands.

Danny cleared his throat, dragging my attention back to him. "Marlee should not have feared her close friend's big brother. He should have been a safe person, and he utterly failed her that night. The moment he laid a hand on her, her life was over. There was no bringing her back."

Danny leaned forward then, with a kind of quiet fury that even scared me a little. "If you choose to believe this monster over a scared girl, then you are a part of the problem. You're telling every other child out there that silence is the answer." He swallowed hard, glancing at the judge. "That's all I've got."

As he stepped down, he didn't look at Adam again. He didn't have to.

He already said what mattered.

He joined us back in the front row of the crowd, blowing out a shaky breath as he did. There was a chorus of 'good job's from our friends, but I couldn't speak.

Because now? Theo was at the witness stand, and his fear was showing far more than the others.

He didn't look at Adam once. Not even a quick glance in his direction.

"I'm here for Marlee," he announced. "Because I believe her, and anybody who doesn't is just as dangerous as *he* is."

His voice didn't shake just yet, but his hands did. He tucked them under the table almost immediately, like he didn't want people to notice his fear.

"I knew Marlee a long time before this happened," he explained, eyes locked on the jury. "When she was loud, and messy, and spent her days talking about the books she read, or the fact that she wanted to be an actor."

His voice dropped as he said, "And I knew her after this. I saw her shrink into herself, and I should have caught the signs." He took a deep breath. "Do you know what it's like to try and live life, to try and wake up every morning, when you've had something like that taken from you?" he asked the jury, shaking his head. "It's a brutal thing to experience, and a brutal thing to drive you to death. This man gave her enough reasons to kill herself at thirteen years old."

He paused, but it wasn't for the jury. It was so he could breathe.

"Marlee McGovern did not lie about this. She couldn't lie." He swallowed hard. "You would be doing the entire world a disjustice to allow this man to live his life. I do not care if he has a bright future ahead of him, or if you believe she was looking for attention. That is sick, and Marlee told the truth. In her last moments, she decided to be brave."

He paused again, blowing out a shaky breath. "If you think this is hard to talk about, imagine living it." He frowned at the crowd, shaking his head rapidly like the weight of this situation was just dawning on him. "Seriously. Imagine fucking living it!"

The judge flinched. The jury chattered worriedly.

Theo continued. "No, no, no. Imagine being stuck in her head while that was replaying every day.

Marlee deserves justice, and I will not be a part of her silence anymore."

The judge pulled him off the witness stand almost instantly, whispering something in his ear that caused him to head to the break room where we were all headed.

Shit.

Theo was holding in so much guilt about failing Marlee that he could barely speak on the stands. I was scared that would happen to me too, but I also knew I couldn't give up. Not now that we'd gotten this far.

Once we were in the break room, each one of us let out a resigned breath.

"I'm sorry," Theo murmured from the head of the table, head dropping to his hands. "I didn't mean to get emotional."

"Do not apologise, Theodore," Liv insisted, taking a seat next to him. "You're allowed to show emotion. We all are." She gestured around the room.

"Thirty minutes 'till we're back on," Danny announced, sounding worried. "You guys think you can handle it?"

"Of course we can," I said, quickly, before anybody else could back out. "For Marlee."

The room was silent when I stepped onto the stand.

This didn't feel real. Being up here, I was so worried about screwing this up for all of us.

I settled into the seat, wishing I could just disappear and teleport to a time where things could be okay.

But I wasn't there.

I never had been

But I *was* here.

And I needed to use my voice, because Marlee was no longer able to.

I didn't look at Adam. I didn't even look at the jury. For now, I kept my eyes locked on Archie, because I knew that was the safest sight. A sight that kept me grounded.

They asked me my name, and I answered.

They asked how I knew Marlee, and I answered.

Then came the question that mattered, and terrified me most: "Why are you here today?"

I dragged in a long breath.

"I'm here because chances are she wasn't the first," I said, voice somehow steady despite the way my entire body wanted to run. "And if he's proven not guilty, she won't have been the last."

I paused, quickly gathering myself before continuing.

Stay strong, Savannah.

I caught Archie's eye from across the room, and I could tell he was proud of me. That was enough for me to continue.

I looked up then, eyes finally locking on the jury. "Marlee McGovern… was the loss of my life," I voiced, hating the way my hands trembled on my lap.

"She was a lot of things, but a liar was *not* one of them."

I took a breath.

"Adam Coleman raped Marlee McGovern," I announced. "I'm not saying that because I want to ruin people's lives, or to take away his future for no reason, or for whatever stupid reasons people like to use when girls are strong enough to tell their truths."

My hands were shaking more obviously now, but I didn't try to stop them. Because I was standing here, and I was honoring my friend who only ever wanted justice. Every damn bone in my body needed to seek justice for that girl. The girl who wouldn't have hesitated to do the same for me.

"Marlee was… everything," I added, biting down on my lip. "She was a lovely girl, and she didn't deserve what happened to her. I'm here today, because I am *begging* you to believe a girl who is forever… *fourteen*."

I stood, walking back down to the crowd, not flinching as I passed Adam. I couldn't give him the satisfaction.

And the worst part? He didn't look remorseful. He didn't look guilty. He didn't even look remotely sad.

He looked evil.

And he *was* evil.

I joined my friends in the front row, immediately sitting down beside Archie. He took my hand right away, giving it a squeeze that gave me the comfort I desperately needed.

Izzie was next, and I was terrified. Because Izzie held everything.

She was the closest to Marlee, she was angry, and she couldn't control herself at times. I could only hope she could keep it together today for Marlee.

Izzie sat in the seat, but she didn't look angry today. She looked defeated, but she didn't let that show for very long.

Izzie always had a way of taking control of rooms, making everyone believe she was the only person in them. But today, in those stands? She looked so small.

She didn't look at the jury. Not at me. Not even at Billy. Definitely not at Adam.

She just picked at the hem of her tee shirt, looking down as if she knew as well as I did she needed to do this. Not for herself, but for Marlee.

Because Marlee McGovern haunted all of us, but she was Izzie's personal ghost.

"Can you tell us how you know Marlee?" Judge Kelly asked, glancing at Izzie.

A small smile twitched on Izzie's lips at the memories, but faded just as quickly. "She was my best friend."

The judge nodded. "How long did you know her?"

"Since we were four," Izzie responded, finally looking at the judge. "We were inseparable."

The judge nodded. "Did you two ever speak about Adam Coleman?"

Izzie hesitated before nodding. "We did. He's our friend Liv's brother, so he was always around."

"And did you believe her when you read this confession in her note?"

Izzie didn't hesitate this time, she just looked offended at the question. "Of course I did."

"Why?"

Izzie scoffed, but quickly regained her composure. "As I said, she was my best friend. I knew when she was telling the truth, and I knew when she was lying. Even on paper."

The judge nodded, seemingly satisfied by her answer. "What would you like to tell the jury, whether regarding Marlee or Adam?"

Izzie glanced at the jury. "I won't say his name, because he makes me sick to my stomach. But Marlee was full of life. She didn't deserve this, and she was *not* lying."

Another pause. Her hands clenched into fists, but she hid them beneath the table. It broke me even further to see how hard she was trying to stay strong, stay calm.

"Marlee didn't survive this," she continued, voice strong despite the obvious hurt. "But I did. That means I will spend my whole life seeking justice for my best friend."

Judge Kelly nodded. "Do you think justice is possible, Miss Harris?"

Izzie lifted her chin, staring at Adam like a blade. "I think justice looks like him being locked up for the rest of his life, unable to hurt anybody else."

That was it.

With that, she was sitting back in our row, hiding the pain I knew she felt deeply.

Izzie Harris didn't have to say much for you to understand her point.

You just did.

Liv moved to the witness stand then, looking every bit as broken and afraid as she deserved to be.

Archie slid his hand into mine once more, clearly noticing my concern. "You did amazing, baby. So will she," he whispered into my ear.

Baby.

Yeah, that was enough to soothe me.

I smiled at his words, returning my attention to where Liv sat at the witness stand.

"Can you state your name for the record?" Judge Kelly asked.

"Olivia Mallory," she whispered, tucking a loose curl behind her ear.

"You're Adam Coleman's younger sister, yes?" Judge Kelly tilted her head. "The record shows that your family adopted him at birth."

Liv swallowed. "That's true."

A few murmurs rippled through the courtroom.

"You were also close with Marlee McGovern, yes?"

Liv's breath caught as she nodded slowly. "She was one of my closest friends."

Judge Kelly nodded, clearly confused by Liv's connection to this case. "And when did you learn about what Adam allegedly did to Marlee?"

"Only a few weeks ago," Liv replied, green eyes locked on the judge as if she couldn't bear to look at anyone else. "Before you ask, no. At first, I didn't believe it, because I didn't want to believe it. When I had a clear head, I believed it immediately, and I vomited. Over and over again. I can't sleep at home anymore."

Liv shook her head, clearly furious at herself for not knowing sooner, even though she wasn't supposed to.

Her eyes locked with Adam's – her own brother – and I could tell she had no sympathy for that man.

Good.

"Marlee was the best part of most of our lives," she said, glaring at him. "And he took her away from us. I will be forever angry."

A long silence followed.

"I hope this shows her that I would have been on her side had she mentioned this alive, and I'm on her side even in her death," Liv continued, rising from her seat. "That's all."

Judge Kelly nodded. "Thank you, Olivia."

Billy was next. Last.

They went through the usual questions, names and what-not.

Once Judge Kelly asked if he knew Adam back then, Billy scoffed bitterly. "Yeah. I knew him."

Judge Kelly arched a brow. "Can you elaborate?"

"We all hung out with the same people." He shifted uncomfortably in his seat, eyes locking on us. "I never felt comfortable with Izzie or anybody else being around him, and I hate to say this isn't much of a surprise to me."

Judge Kelly nodded along.

"It's devastating," Billy continued. "And I have nothing more to say, other than I hope Adam rots in hell for the rest of his life."

Once the testimonies were over, we all sat in the front row, nervous for the results.

My hands were wrung together on my lap, panic rushing through my veins.

He had to be convicted, right?

Right?

"There is no way he won't be found as guilty," Archie whispered in my ear, clearly catching onto my worries. "You'll see."

The silence when the jury was taken out for the decision was colder than anything I'd seen today.

The jury filed back into the room with unreadable expressions. The judge looked exhausted, like she'd aged twenty years in a day. Everybody around me held their breaths, or held hands with somebody else.

I held tighter onto Archie's hand, panic surging through me like never before.

He had to be found guilty.

He *had* to be.

"Will the defendant please rise."

Adam stood. There was no fear in his eyes, just cruel certainty.

That scared me a little more.

I didn't blink once. Archie's hand was holding onto mine like a lifeline, a look of uncertainty on his face worrying me further.

Izzie was holding Billy's hand. Theo was holding Liv's. Danny, for whatever reason, was holding Josie's.

The jury foreperson stood.

"In the matter of The State vs. Adam Coleman…"

A pause.

The moment the world stopped spinning.

I think I stopped breathing for a moment, but I didn't care.

This was it.

"We find the defendant… not guilty."

Silence.

Then breaths of disbelief.

Then… chaos.

Izzie flipped a chair. Or threw it at Adam. I wasn't sure. I was still in shock.

I could hear sobs and screams from behind me.

Izzie didn't say a word. She just stood up and left as if she'd already rehearsed this. As always, Billy followed straight after her.

"They let him walk," Danny muttered, shaking his head in utter disbelief. "They let him walk. Fuck."

Theo and Liv rushed out just as Josie and Danny did.

I couldn't move. It was like my feet were stuck in place.

Lila McGovern collapsed into her chair, sobbing like a small child. There was nothing anybody could do, or say to undo what had just been done. Her daughter's voice never mattered. Not to them.

Fuck.

And Adam?

He stood up, smirked, and walked out.

As if he'd won.

No, he had won.

He won.

Involuntarily, I broke into sobs, collapsing into Archie's arms. "Shit," I whispered through the tears. "Shit."

CAN'T CATCH ME NOW

OCTOBER 11TH 2004

SAVANNAH

Not guilty.

Not guilty

Not guilty.

Not guilty.

Not guilty.

The words pulsed in my mind like a warning light that wouldn't turn off no matter how hard I tried.

"Savvy?" a small voice whispered, dragging me away from my sleep.

I opened my eyes, blinking a few times to check who was in my bed. When my eyes were clear, I saw Aidan on my lap. He looked so small, so worried.

"Are you okay, baby?" I asked, pulling him in for a hug.

It didn't matter that we had a safe family now. I was those boy's mum, and that didn't stop simply because it wasn't necessary anymore.

Aidan nodded once. "You were making the sad face again."

I frowned at his words, hating that he could tell, because there was no proper explanation I could give him. "Was I, bud?"

He nodded again, looking into my eyes with a deep level of trust. "Did you have a bad dream?"

I smiled up at him. "A very bad one."

"They not real, Savvy," Aidan whispered, hugging me tightly. "The monsters just like to scare you."

I nodded. "I know, buddy. I'm okay."

Aidan smiled as I said that, not looking worried anymore. "I had a bad dream too."

"You did?" I asked, worried. I brushed his blonde hair back, searching his eyes. I didn't like the fact that he was still afraid, even in sleep.

Aidan nodded in confirmation. "Daddy found me, Savvy. It was so scary."

I sat up further, looking into his eyes with sincerity. "You know it was only a bad dream, right?"

"Yeah," he agreed sadly. "But he was so mean."

"Hey," I whispered, smiling with as much enthusiasm as possible. "Daddy wasn't a nice man. But now, guess what? You have Jason, and he loves you so much."

"Can he be my dad?" he asked innocently. "I want him to be."

My smile stretched wider. "Of course he can."

"Hey, Sav?" my baby brother said, thoughtfully. "Who's that boy you're always with? The one with the scary eyes."

"Scary eyes?" I repeated, huffing a laugh. "Archie doesn't have scary eyes."

"Archie," he whispered, more to himself than me. "He's so nice, Savvy. But his eyes are so green."

I chuckled. "You don't like that?"

Aidan thought for a moment. "I like him if he's nice to you, Savvy."

I pulled him closer, wanting to protect him from the world.

But I realised something.

He didn't need protection anymore.

And life wasn't as bad as it felt, because the boys were safe. *My* boys were safe.

And Archie... he wanted to be with me.

RAMBLING IN LOVE

OCTOBER 16TH 2004

ARCHIE

Sav was laying across my chest, and neither of us had spoken for a while.

She showed up an hour ago without notice, and we'd been laying in my bed ever since. I wasn't sure why she was here, but I couldn't complain. I wanted her around, *always*.

Especially in times like these.

I hadn't expected her to show up today considering she'd only left my house this morning after a well-needed group sleepover, but I was glad she'd come back.

Maybe it was selfish, but I wanted to keep her.

Just for me.

It didn't matter that one day I'd have to fly overseas for basketball.

If she wanted me to stay? I would stay without a thought. And if she wanted to join me in France? I'd pay for those tickets immediately.

I just couldn't lose this girl.

And nothing else mattered more.

"Sav?" I finally whispered, running my hand through her crazy brown hair. "How are you doing?"

"Everything's different," she replied, head resting on my chest. "Everyone, everything is changing."

"I know," I replied quietly.

"He shouldn't get to walk." Shaking her head, she lifted herself up. "I know it doesn't affect me like it might other people, but it's just not fair." She sighed, looking into my eyes. "If my Dad hadn't died, and he'd gotten caught, I would be devastated if he was declared not guilty."

"I know," I replied, because she didn't need my input. She just needed me to listen. All she ever wanted was somebody to listen, and I'd be that for her. I'd be *everything* for her.

"It's not fair on Liv," she continued with a frown. "Or Marlee's Mum. I don't know. It just doesn't sit right with me."

"It's not right," I agreed, voice quiet and understanding. "But we can't change what the court decided."

"I know." She nodded, smiling slightly. "I still wish we could."

I blew out a shaky breath, deciding to offer some personal insight. "They never caught the man who was speeding the night my Dad and Elsie died."

That caught her attention. Her eyes widened, tilting her head as she listened to my every word. "What do you mean?"

"Dad only swerved because a car was coming full speed down the other lane," I explained, flinching at the memories that flashed through my mind. "If that driver had been going at the right speed limit, they would have lived."

She frowned. "That's really bad, Archie."

"I know." I nodded in agreement. "I was angry, because they hardly even tried to catch him. But my point is, it's not fair. It's fucking bullshit. But you can't change it, and neither could I."

She smiled sympathetically. "You don't talk about it enough. You don't talk about it ever."

I let out a weak chuckle at her words. "I thought I'd die, Sav. I wasn't ready to die, and I wasn't ready to watch them die, either."

She frowned, pressing a soft kiss to my cheek. "I'm sorry, Archie."

"It was a long time ago."

"What was it you said to me?" She pretended to think for a moment, tapping her chin. "Trauma doesn't have an expiration date."

"And I stand by that," I told her. "But I had people to help me through it. You lived your whole life without ever telling anybody what you were going through." I frowned at the thought of her living through that alone, and made a vow to myself that I'd never allow her to be alone again. "You definitely don't give yourself enough credit."

That got a small smile out of her. "No, I didn't tell anyone. But that didn't mean I was alone. I always had Liv, Izzie, and Josie."

"Still."

She shook her head. "Izzie was wonderful, Archie. I know you don't like her because of Theo, and that's okay. But my childhood would have been worse had Izzie not been my close friend."

"Yeah?" I tilted my head, suddenly a bit thankful for the demon girl that had made my best friend's life a living hell.

We were silent for a moment.

Then, I added, "I'm so fucking sorry, Sav. You'll never understand how badly I wish I knew."

"You stayed," she told me, smiling. "That was the best thing you could have done with what you knew."

I blew out a long sigh. "I wish I could have done more."

"Keep staying," she advised, sounding worried. "I don't know how to believe that you're not gonna run at the first sight of danger."

I frowned at that. "I don't do this, Sav. I have never, in my life, been with a girl that I had genuine feelings for," I explained, keeping my voice calm despite the way that I wanted to scream and beg her to believe me. "And you're different. When I say something to you, I mean it. You best believe I'm not going anywhere, Sav."

That got her smiling again, then she pressed her lips to mine.

Unable to take another moment of doubt with this girl, I deepened the kiss, pulling her in closer to my chest.

Her hands found their way to my back, sliding beneath my shirt just enough to feel my skin. And she didn't stop.

I wanted her. Fuck, I wanted her.

But this was Sav.

And if I knew anything, I knew I needed to be more careful than ever when it came to this girl.

I didn't want to stop, but her hands were exploring further, and I knew stopping was the only option.

Because I knew this girl. It was like her body was asking, but her mind and heart hadn't quite caught up yet. I knew when her laugh was real and when it was a show, and I certainly knew when her determination was actually fear of not doing something right.

So, I pulled back.

"Sav," I said softly, still a bit breathless. "You know I want you, right? And I want this."

"Why did you stop?" she asked, eyes wider and more vulnerable than I'd ever seen them.

"Because I also know you're not ready for this," I told her. "Not yet."

Her eyes widened, and for a moment, I thought she might walk away. But she didn't. Instead, she exhaled a breath like she'd been holding it forever.

"I don't wanna disappoint you," she whispered sadly, hand resting on my cheek.

"You are doing anything but disappointing me," I assured her, voice calm despite the million fucking thoughts rushing through my mind. "This only means something if we're both ready, Sav. Not just one of us."

She smiled.

"I'll wait forever if that's what you need," I told her, feeling a desperate need to comfort her. "I might lose my mind waiting, but I'll wait."

She exhaled another sigh. "Thank you, Archie."

Even though every cell in my body was screaming for more, I didn't move. Didn't push. I just kept my arms wrapped around her, knowing this was the right decision for now.

"I love you," she blurted out suddenly, shaking her head as she spoke. "Yeah, it's very soon to say that. But, you know what? We've been dancing around this since the start of the year, and I can't—" She paused for a second, catching her breath. Then, "And I love you. I do. So, so much. Everything else is terrible, but you're right here. Right in front of me. And... yeah. I love you."

When she finished, she looked up at me with those wide, grey eyes I'd been fucking obsessed with since February, and bit down nervously on her lip.

I smiled in reassurance. "I love you too, Sav. Of course I do."

She exhaled a breath of relief. "Good, because that would have been really awkward if it went the other way."

I huffed a laugh. "I suppose we'll never know, hm?"

She grinned. "I hope not."

"Were you different?" I suddenly asked, tilting my head to properly look into her eyes.

"What?"

"Before everything happened. You know? Marlee, before everything got worse at home, before... everything," I explained, curious. "Were you different?"

"Yeah," she whispered, nodding once. "I think I was different. Especially before Marlee died. But that girl couldn't defend herself." She shrugged, smiling down at me. "She was helpless and lonely."

I frowned at those words, feeling an indescribable need to protect this girl with my life. "You're not alone anymore, Sav. You know that, right?"

"Yeah, baby," she replied with a soft smile, hand drifting back to my cheek. "I know that."

And, apparently, this girl knew no bounds. Wrapping her arms around my neck, she pulled me in for a kiss deeper than before.

After a while, she pulled away. "Archie," she whispered. "Please."

Fucking hell.

See, self-restraint had never been a problem of mine.

I was always good at knowing exactly what I should and shouldn't do.

But, fuck, she made it a whole lot harder.

"Sav," I whispered back, fighting with my entire body not to give in. Not until I knew she was sure.

"No regrets." She smiled sweetly, reaching for the waistband of my jeans.

Yeah, I knew I had no choice in the matter anymore.

"We're not having sex tonight," I warned, feeling a need to at least stay firm on that. "But I can do something else if you want."

Her eyes lit up, causing me to huff a laugh.

Her fingers traced slow circles along my belt buckle, eyes locked onto mine with that daring glint I couldn't resist. "Something else sounds perfect," she whispered, voice low and a little breathless.

I swallowed hard, the heat between us undeniable. "Like what?" I teased, inching closer, the space between us shrinking with every heartbeat.

She smiled, mischievous and soft all at once. "You're the one making the rules here."

I pulled her closer, our bodies barely apart. The heat between us was electric, a fire ready to ignite. My hand slid to the small of her back, pulling her flush against me.

She gasped, and I kissed the spot just beneath her ear, letting my breath ghost over her skin. "Tell me what you want, Sav," I murmured, "and I'll make sure you get it."

Instead of using words, the little spark of TNT slid my hand just beneath the waistband of her skirt. "You tell me."

Mia Jade

ALL SORTS OF RIGHT

OCTOBER 23RD 2004

SAVANNAH

Archie Bennett, somehow, made me happier than anybody else ever had.

It was entirely unexpected, and last year, I would have laughed at those words.

But I had no doubt about him.

The world was cruel, and I knew that fact better than anybody. But, you know what? It didn't feel so disappointing with this boy by my side.

It felt all sorts of right.

"What movie are we watching?" Josie asked, strolling into our local cinemas.

"Vanity Fair," Liv answered without hesitation, smiling brightly as she glanced at Theo.

"We saw that last week," Theo answered, glaring at Liv. "Are there seriously no other movies you'd enjoy, Livvy?"

"Nope," Liv answered sweetly, smiling up at the curly-haired blonde boy. "Just this one."

Theo chuckled, but I knew he'd give in. It was Liv, after all. "Okay, Livvy. Only for you."

Archie smiled down at me, fingers entwined with mine. "You ready?"

My eyes darted around, counting all of our friends to make sure we weren't missing anybody. "Yep. Danny got the tickets."

Archie smiled, swaying our hands slightly as we all made our way into the cinema. He leaned down to whisper in my ear. "You tell me if it gets too much, okay?"

"I can handle movies," I teased.

He rolled his eyes. "I know that. Can you handle the people we're watching it with?"

"Ah," I replied, nodding at his words. "Let's see."

We strolled in, seeing the movie had already started playing a few minutes ago. We only missed the opening, so it was okay.

But in all honesty?

I didn't care about the movie.

Sure, movies were fun and all, but I was here because everyone that had made my life bearable was.

That mattered the most.

We took our seats in the back, basically taking up the whole row.

I squeezed in between Archie and Izzie, allowing my eyes to dart up to the screen. Allowing myself to enjoy the little things in life.

A few minutes later, I caught Izzie glancing at me. She looked up a few times, but looked back down to her feet after a second.

"Izzie," I whispered, keeping my voice quiet. "Are you okay?"

She shrugged, not quite meeting my eyes. "All good, Sav."

I eyed her, not believing that for a moment. "Are you sure?"

"Aren't I always?" Was her response. Then, "I'll be just fine, Sav. I always am."

I bit down on my lip, unsure of whether I should push for the truth. When anyone else pushed her, she snapped. But with me? She was never like that.

Izzie with me was different to Izzie with everybody else.

"You can talk to me, Izzie." I decided to say, hoping to comfort her without prying too much. "Always."

That earned a half-smile from her. "I know that."

I nodded, satisfied enough with her answer.

I leant back in my chair, allowing my head to rest on Archie's shoulder when he pulled me in closer.

I closed my eyes for a moment. Just one. Just long enough to breathe in the faint scent of popcorn, and listen to the movie tracks playing in the background. Long enough to feel that little bit of peace that I never believed I deserved. Never believed I'd find.

A few seats down, Liv was whispering something into Theo's ear. I could only guess she was rambling on about the movie, things he'd heard a million times, because he scoffed at her words. The smile twitching on his lips gave him away, though.

He was hopeless for her, and everybody knew it. Everybody had known it for years.

Josie passed the popcorn to Danny, nearly dropping it into his lap, which earned an exaggerated sigh from him.

I smiled.

These people.

This moment.

Somehow, in the midst of all the drama, all the grief, and all the heartbreak, we always had this. While this group wasn't always peaceful, they were always my comfort. *My* home.

I could hear the others talking, but I couldn't make it out. Theo muttered something after Izzie did. I still couldn't understand against the noise of the movie, but Izzie caught it.

And I saw it.

The way her hands balled into fists, the way she was visibly attempting to keep her mouth closed, the way her eyes went wild and crazy.

And I hated it.

Because Izzie wasn't mean.

Izzie was just sick.

And nobody seemed to quite understand that.

She stormed out of the room a few seconds later, with Billy and Danny following closely behind like service dogs.

The others went quiet after that, but something in Izzie's eyes told me it was worse this time. *She* was worse this time.

I felt so helpless staying here, but I knew I wasn't what she needed.

Billy was who she needed.

I shifted uncomfortably in my seat, leaning in closer to Archie's touch. The one touch that never made me believe danger came after it.

We were sitting on the bridge between safety and the chaos around us, and still, the safety one when he was near.

Because whether he knew it or not, Archie was the one to save me when I believed it was impossible.

And when I closed my eyes, I could see it. That future I'd never been able to picture.

Yeah, I could see it clearly now.

And Archie was in it.

Just like he promised.

"Should we get going?" he whispered in my ear, clearly as uncomfortable as I was.

I nodded immediately. "Let's go."

I wasn't sure how this kept happening.

Before Archie, I'd never even kissed a boy. I was very behind in that area, to say the least.

But now? Well, I kept ending up in his bed, laying below him as he kissed me.

Yeah, it happened *again*.

I kissed him back, deepening it with as much strength as possible. I couldn't quite put it into words, but I wanted to stay like this forever. I never, ever wanted to let him go.

His hands found my waist, holding me like I might disappear if he didn't. Maybe I would have. In some ways, I had spent my whole life disappearing.

But now?

I wasn't a ghost watching the world go by.

I was living.

He pulled me closer, our bodies flush. It was like everything else around us just… faded.

The chaos. The drama. The sadness. The worry.

They all turned into background thoughts, and my mind was entirely focused on the boy hovering over me.

Our clothes didn't take long to be discarded, and I was more than happy about it.

My fingers tangled in his hair, and his breath hitched as I deepened the kiss. It felt like we were speaking in a secret language that nobody else understood, and it was all I ever wanted to speak from now on. Forever.

I felt it.

All of it.

So strongly.

The hope. The want. The excitement.

But then, he slowed. Nothing obvious, just a slight pause in the kiss. A falter in his movements.

"Archie," I whispered, utterly desperate. "I want this. I really, really do."

Last time was perfect.

But it wasn't enough.

And I needed all of him.

His hand moved to cup my face, looking at me with tender concern. "Hey. Slow down, baby. No need to rush."

"But I want you."

His breath hitched. "I want you too. More than anything."

"Please," I whispered, pulling him in closer.

He tried to hide it, but I could see the way his resolve started to waver. "You're making it really hard to be responsible."

"So don't be responsible."

He groaned, lips finding my neck. "I don't think I can say no to you."

I managed a soft laugh. "You don't want to say no to me."

"No, I don't," he admitted.

"Stop worrying, then." I smiled up at him.

For a moment, he hesitated, but it didn't take long until he was unclasping my bra. "I'll try. Just promise me you'll tell me if you want to stop at any point."

"I promise."

He kissed his way down my chest, his touch becoming more confident. "Okay."

I sighed in relief. "Thank you."

He paused to look into my eyes. "I think I'm the lucky one here, Sav."

"I need to make sure you're one hundred percent certain," he mumbled, voice rough with restraint. "I don't want to hurt you, and I don't want you to regret this." His fingers traced gentle patterns over my thighs, working their way slowly upward, yet remaining at a respectful distance. A *painful* distance, because I needed him closer.

"Archie, I'm sure. I want this," I assured him, nodding. "Please. I want *you*."

He searched my eyes one more time, as if he was making sure I was *absolutely* sure.

When he found no signs of uncertainty, he kissed me deeply, slowly entering my body. "I love you," he whispered against my swollen lips, his body trembling with the obvious effort of being gentle. "God, I love you so much."

"I love you too."

WORDS I CANNOT SAY

OCTOBER 25TH 2004

SAVANNAH

Dear Marlee,

I know you won't get this, and that fact kills me more than I can explain. While I don't believe in any sort of heaven, I can only hope that you're watching over me.

If you are, and wherever you are, I hope that you're proud of me.

Sometimes I like to believe that you're just on a really long holiday, and not actually gone. Gone doesn't make sense, Mar. Gone is too far away.

I want to believe that you are proud. Even though I make mistakes, I hope that you watch over me every day. That thought keeps me going most days.

We really tried with the trial, Mar. I promise.

It was hard to stand up there and fight, but I kept going, because I knew I was doing it for you, and I knew I needed to be strong since that chance was taken away from you.

I promise you, Marlee, the fight is not over. I will make sure the whole world knows your name, your story. I will fight until the very end to make sure justice is served.

For a while after you left, I had to keep convincing myself there would be happiness after you. At the time, it seemed like a silly and impossible thought. Back then, there was no happiness. There was just silence.

Sometimes, you still haunt me. Sometimes, I see you everywhere, in everything. I know you did what you felt was the best choice for you, and I'll never be angry at you for that, but I wish you had other options. I wish you were here.

Marlee, I don't feel so lost anymore.

Do you remember Archie Bennett? Somehow, I'm dating him. You'd probably be shocked if you were here, and I was too. It was really unexpected, but it's been amazing.

People still talk about you sometimes. Archie likes to know more about you, and our friends still miss you, even if they keep it to themselves a lot.

There were a few times last year where I wanted to give up and just come join you. I understood how it felt like you're only out.

I thank you for writing the letters you did, because they've helped. So much.

Not only with seeking justice for your name, but also with the healing process. It took me a long time to read it, but it means a lot to have it.

Sometimes, when I miss you the most, I just have to read your words again. They hurt a lot, Marlee, but they also make me happy, because that's the last thing I have of you.

Some days, it does still feel impossible without you here. Living life without you never felt like something I'd have to do. Now that it is, it feels strange, like a piece of me was taken the night you died.

Izzie misses you. She doesn't say it much, but it's obvious. She isn't the same anymore, Mar. She wants her best friend back.

I like to hope that she and Billy get their happy ending. I hope that she can heal and see herself the way you always did, the way I do. If that ever happens, I'll write another letter.

Everybody else is doing the best that they can.

Liv is confused about the whole situation, but she believes you, Mar. She believes you with everything she has, even though it's unraveled her whole life.

I need you to know something: if you had told us when you were alive, none of us would have hesitated to believe you. We all would've, and we would've fought for you.

Again, I don't blame you for the way things panned out. It wasn't your fault, but I still wish I could have saved you.

I'll never stop missing you, Mar. But I need to learn how to live my life without the grief weighing me down.

This isn't goodbye. Not really.

I will love you forever, my girl.

-   *Savannah.*

CAMPING AND FEELINGS

OCTOBER 30TH 2004

ARCHIE

"That is a *really* big spider," Sav shrieked from beside me. She looked up at me, eyes wide. "I can't believe you made me go camping again. You know how I feel about those wild animals."

I chuckled. "What wild animals?"

"The bears," Sav said, the look in her eyes telling me she well and truly believed 'the bears' would come attack her. "And those disgusting spiders, Archie!"

I laughed uncontrollably now. She probably hated me, but I couldn't help it.

She gasped, shoving me half-playfully half-seriously. "Do you really find my fear so funny?"

"What bears are you afraid of, Sav?" I asked, trying my hardest not to laugh again.

"All of them, obviously." She rolled her eyes, then glared at me. "What, you're telling me you aren't afraid of bears?"

"I'm telling you Australia doesn't have bears," I told her between chuckles. "Jesus, Sav."

Her eyes widened, looking genuinely surprised. "Then why am I so scared of them?"

I ran a hand down my face, huffing another laugh. "Couldn't tell ya. Not much of a camper, huh?"

"The first time I went camping was Liv's birthday," she explained, eyes darting around the campsite. "And I was just as terrified then."

I rolled my eyes, zipping up the tent. "I'll protect you."

"Thanks." She smiled sweetly, still suspicious.

"Stop looking at me like that." I smirked, chuckling as she frowned up at me. "I didn't create spiders."

She shivered. "Don't talk about them."

I pretended to think for a moment, then pressed a lingering kiss to her forehead. "Fine. If you say so."

"I do say so." She crossed her arms over her chest, but her smile gave her away.

"I love you, Savannah Grey," I told her, smiling lovingly. "Always and forever."

"You're sweet." Her smile stretched, and she moved closer to me. "And I love you more."

Pausing thoughtfully, she rested her head on my shoulder. "Do you think Marlee would be proud of me?"

"Absolutely," I answered without hesitation.

"You think the others will be okay?" she asked.

"We're all getting there," I said softly, pulling her closer. "Bit by bit."

She smiled against me, warmth settling over us both.

"Promise me something?" she whispered.

I smiled, knowing there was nothing in the world I wouldn't do for this girl."Anything."

"Don't leave." She tilted her head. "Even if the fancy basketballer people want you. Even if it gets hard or messy. Don't let go."

I kissed her temple. "I promise."

She kissed me softly, then pulled back to look into my eyes. "You saved my life, Archie Bennett. Thank you."

"No thanking me," I whispered, unwilling to take all the credit when this girl was stronger than anybody I'd met before. "Besides, I think healing *you* healed *me* too."

Acknowledgements

Hi! I've been dying to write Archie and Savannah's second book since the moment I began planning this series, and it became exactly what I hoped for. Thank you to each and every one of you who took the time to read Healing You, and I hope you enjoyed it as much as I did.

I'd like to thank a few extra special people who made this journey one to remember.

Mum and John, thank you for believing in me even when I didn't, and for making me believe this was possible.

Laura, thank you for being one of my biggest supporters and cheerleaders for the whole process. I genuinely could not have done this without you.

And for my readers, I'll never stop appreciating you endlessly! Thank you for reading, and I hope you'll stick along for the ride.

Songs for Savannah

Taylor swift - "Mastermind"
Paris Paloma - "Labour"
Taylor Swift - "The Archer"
Olivia Rodrigo - "Making The Bed"
Susannah Joffe - "Die Your Daughter"
Gracie Abrams - "Block Me Out"
Harry Styles - "Matilda"
Conan Gray - "Family Line"
Phoebe Bridgers - "Funeral"
Billie Eilish - "Getting Older"
Taylor Swift - "The Great War"
Billie Eilish - "Blue"
Taylor Swift - "Mirrorball"
Gracie Abrams - "Long Sleeves"
Cults - "Gilded Lily"
Taylor swift - "Seven"
Mitski - "I Bet On Losing Dogs"
The Marias - "No One Noticed"
Taylor Swift - "I Hate It Here"
Renee Rapp - "Snow Angel"
Taylor Swift - "Long Story Short"
Maroon 5 - "She Will Be Loved"
Taylor Swift - "When Emma Falls In Love"
The Fray - "How To Save A Life"
Conan Gray - "Fight or Flight"

Mitski - "A Burning Hill"
Taylor Swift - "So High School"
Taylor Swift - "You Are In Love"
Mazzy Star - "Fade Into You"
Phoebe Bridgers - "Motion Sickness"
Florence + The Machine - "Never Let Me Go"
Taylor Swift - "My Tears Ricochet"
Taylor Swift - "Begin Again"
Olivia Rodrigo - "Brutal"

Songs for Archie

Wheatus - "Teenage Dirtbag"
The Fray - "Look After You"
Taylor Swift - "All Of The Girls You Loved Before"
Cigarettes After Sex - "Nothing's Gonna Hurt You Baby"
Gracie Abrams - "Feels Like"
The Police - "Every Breath You Take"
Kids That Fly - "Kiss Her You Fool"
Robbie Williams - "Angels"
Frankie Valli - "Can't Take My Eyes off You"
KISS - "I Was Made For Lovin' You"
Halsey - "Bad At Love"
Ed Sheeran - "Photograph"
Snow Patrol - "Chasing Cars"
Lewis Capaldi - "Before You Go"
Keane - "Somewhere Only We Know"
Coldplay - "Fix You"
The Script - "The Man Who Can't Be Moved"
The National - "I Need My Girl"
Angus & Julia Stone - "Big Jet Plane"

www.ingramcontent.com/pod-product-compliance
Lightning Source LLC
Chambersburg PA
CBHW022141170626
46807CB00005B/2032